"Gemma, you're going to be as beautiful as—"

Ben had come very close to saying Sera, Gemma's identical twin, the sister he'd used as a model in his reconstructive surgery of Gemma's face.

He quickly substituted, "As you always are."

It touched him to see tears fill her eyes and trickle down her cheeks. He put a comforting hand on her shoulder. To his shock and dismay, she instantly threw herself at him, wrapping her arms around his neck, pressing her body against him in an overtly sexual way.

As gently as possible, Ben unhooked her arms and moved a discreet distance away.

She fumbled in her purse, pulled out a folded paper and thrust it at him.

Ben unfolded it, and as he read quickly through it, horror and disbelief overwhelmed him. Certain phrases reverberated like bombshells in his brain:

I know how much you want to make your feelings for me clear.... I feel the same. Can't wait until you're no longer just my doctor.... Never loved anyone this much before.

Having a patient make a pass was a physician's worst nightmare. It could so easily be mishandled, resulting in nasty allegations of sexual misconduct. But what really appalled him was that the pass was coming from Sera's sister.

Sera, the woman he loved.

Dear Reader,

There was a time not long ago when only Hollywood stars had plastic surgery to change the way they looked. Now it's commonplace; everybody's doing it. Who among us hasn't looked in the mirror, felt dissatisfied and fantasized about how we'd like to have this less bumpy or that less baggy?

But how would it feel to suddenly have that familiar face in the mirror smashed beyond recognition? What would it do to our sense of who we are and what we are? And what if the face we were born with also belonged to an identical twin? These are the questions that marked the genesis of this book.

Too often, we think of plastic surgery only in terms of vanity, of a tuck here or a nip there, forgetting the work done in reconstructing accidental injury and congenital deformity. Too often, we focus on physical appearance and forget, as Shakespeare said, that "Love looks not with the eyes but with the mind, and therefore is winged Cupid painted blind."

I hope you enjoy reading these medical books as much as I enjoy writing them.

Bobby Hutchinson

WOMAN IN THE MIRROR
Bobby Hutchinson

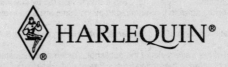

HARLEQUIN®

TORONTO • NEW YORK • LONDON
AMSTERDAM • PARIS • SYDNEY • HAMBURG
STOCKHOLM • ATHENS • TOKYO • MILAN • MADRID
PRAGUE • WARSAW • BUDAPEST • AUCKLAND

ISBN 0-373-70906-4

WOMAN IN THE MIRROR

Printed in U.S.A.

For advice on Gemma's reconstruction, thank you, Dr. Brian Peterson. Thanks, too, to Dr. J. Scott Williamson for information on reconstructive plastic surgery.

Thanks, as always, to Dr. Greg McCloskey and to Patricia Gibson, who endlessly and patiently answer my questions and suggest brilliant solutions.

And to my lawyer, Trudy Hopman-Jackart, who also happens to be my daughter-in-law, so many thanks for professional advice regarding my characters.

CHAPTER ONE

"OKAY, CHARLES, let's take these dressings off and you'll feel a whole lot better."

Reconstructive surgeon Ben Halsey gently began to unwind the yards of gauze he'd used to protect his handiwork. Two days before, he'd performed aesthetic surgery on sixty-two-year-old Charles Bedford, both blepharoplasty to remove the pouches under his eyes, and rhytidectomy, a full face-lift to eliminate the wrinkles and sagging skin on his face and neck. The procedures had taken just over five hours in the OR, and Ben knew the results would be all that Charles had hoped for, but at the moment his patient's bruised and swollen face looked anything but handsome.

The last piece of gauze fell away, and Charles's flattened and blood-matted cap of silver hair appeared. Ben liked his patient's attitude. When he'd asked Charles during the preliminary visits why he wanted the surgery, the man had grinned wryly and said that obviously it wasn't just because he wanted to look younger; if that was the case, he'd have dyed his hair long ago. No, he wanted to *feel* more youthful, he'd explained; there was a difference. But appearance was important, too. He was a businessman, an executive at a large insurance company. Looking his best might help him make vice president before he retired.

Until a few years ago, Ben had done this type of surgery predominantly on women. In the past several years, he'd had an increasing number of men requesting cosmetic procedures, so now the numbers of men and women were almost equal. It was an interesting comment on society's changing attitudes.

"You're gonna look at least ten years younger when this swelling goes down," he assured Charles.

"That'll be about ten years older than you, then," his patient joked. "Why is it you doctors look so young?"

"Because we *are* young." Ben laughed, not bothering to tell his patient he was actually even younger than Charles had guessed. He knew that certain mornings he appeared much older than his thirty-six years; Charles must have based his assessment of Ben's age on one of those bad days, guessing him at forty-two.

Yet the nights preceding those mornings were delectable. Sex might not make him look younger, Ben mused, but it certainly contributed to a youthful attitude.

"Aaaggghhh." Charles grimaced and his hands clenched.

"Sorry, sorry, just one more and we're done here." Ben was now deftly extricating the last of the small, thin tubes he'd placed behind each ear to allow the blood collecting under the skin to drain. "These sutures are looking good." He'd closed the incisions along the natural skin lines and creases so they'd be all but invisible. He tipped his patient's chin up gently to check the two-inch incision that had facilitated the liposuction device to remove the accumulation of fat from the neck. Ben had also tightened the muscles and connective tissue in the area, pulling the loose skin up and back, tailoring it to the face, suturing it in front of and behind the ears and snipping off the excess.

"I want you to wear this supportive bandage at night and as much as possible during the day for the next ten days. The swelling and skin discoloration will subside within a week or two. You may have some numbness in your face for a while, but that'll disappear. Healing's a gradual process, with final results not fully realized for three to six weeks."

Charles nodded. Ben had covered all this before the surgery. "I'm so damned itchy. I can't wait to have a shower and shampoo."

"I don't know—I sort of like the punk look," Ben joked. He enjoyed making his patients smile.

"For a few months I want you to stay out of the sun, and after that use a sunscreen with a high protective factor when you go sailing." Charles had confided that he had a forty-two-foot sailboat.

"Sunscreen won't be an issue unless Vancouver's weather changes drastically," Charles remarked. It had been raining steadily all through the first half of June.

There was a discreet tap at the door, and Ben's office nurse, Dana Dolgoff, stuck her head in.

"Emergency over at St. Joe's, Doctor. They want you there stat."

"Okay, Dana. We're done here. Come back in two days and we'll see about those sutures, Charles. Dana, I'll call and tell you whether we need to cancel this afternoon's appointments."

"Right, Doctor." Dana nodded with a dubious expression on her friendly face. She didn't believe him. She knew he'd get so involved he'd forget. She'd been with him since he'd opened his private practice three years before, and she understood him as well as any female.

"I *will* call this time. Honest. I'm working on responsibility this week," he teased her as he grabbed his pager and his navy raincoat and loped out the door, down the stairs of the professional building and out into the heavy rain.

Having an office situated right across the street from St. Joseph's Medical Center was well worth the exorbitant rent the space cost him. It meant that he could be in Emerg within six minutes of a call. Face-lifts and nose jobs were great because they paid the bills, but the unexpected challenges, the high drama in St. Joe's Emerg, were what Ben lived for. Those, and his dream of heading the burn unit that would be housed in the new wing presently under construction at the back of St. Joe's.

He was hoping for a sessional appointment, which would mean he'd spend a fixed portion of his workweek at the burn unit, with adequate time left over to devote to his private practice.

He strode to the crosswalk and held up a peremptory hand to a bus. When it groaned to a halt, he stepped out into the bumper-to-bumper traffic on Burrard Street, adrenaline coursing through his veins. Three minutes later, the wide automatic doors to the ER parted to allow him through.

The triage nurse, Leslie Yates, hurried toward him.

"Hi, Dr. Halsey. You got here fast."

"Like a speeding bullet. What've you got for me, Les?" He shucked off his raincoat and tossed it behind the nurses' desk. The nurses knew him. One of them would hang it up for him. He used a corner of his shirt to wipe the rain from his wire-rimmed glasses before plunking them back on his nose.

"Bad one, Doctor. Young female construction worker on the hospital project, hit in the face with a two-by-four being moved by a forklift.'' As she spoke, she quickly led the way to trauma room three. ''The good news is, she was working just outside the hospital, so we got her in here right away. Her name's Gemma Cardano.''

A large burly man with steel-gray hair was standing at the bank of phones, anguish on his strongly drawn features as he spoke urgently into the mouthpiece, punctuating his words with dramatic hand gestures.

''That's her father, Aldo Cardano,'' Leslie explained in a quiet tone. ''He's the contractor on the construction project. And that tall man sitting over there is the one who was operating the forklift. He's pretty shaken up. I should speak to him. Excuse me, Ben.'' She moved away.

Ben paused outside the door to the trauma room only long enough to scrub and put on a gown and mask. Inside, senior ER physician Joanne Duncan greeted him and rapidly gave him a summary of her findings.

''Twenty-nine-year-old female with multiple facial fractures—unstable zygomatic process, fractured nose, fractured mandible. Pupillary response sluggish. Airways clear. We did a C-spine precaution. That was fine. Patient is conscious.''

Ben listened intently, his attention centered on the slender figure on the gurney. What Joanne was describing was an injury so severe it could be fatal,

the dreaded Lafort three, which meant that the entire bone structure of the face—nose, cheekbones
and jaw—was unsteady. Breathing was often jeop-
ardized; loss of vision was a very real possibility if
the bones that surrounded the eyes, called the floor
of the orbit, were involved. There was a danger of
total loss of the olfactory sense and a compromised
ability to chew, swallow and talk.

His adrenaline surged anew and anticipation
filled him. This was exactly the sort of case he
found most fulfilling.

Ben leaned over the figure on the gurney.
''Gemma, I'm Dr. Ben Halsey, a reconstructive surgeon. I'm just having a look at you.'' He spoke
calmly, doing his own fast but thorough assessment
of the injuries, moving aside gauze to reveal a nasty
gash on the right side of the face where the edge
of the board had struck.

She was making an agonizing sound that ema-
nated from somewhere deep in her chest. Her curly
golden-brown hair was long and wild; the nurses
had secured it away from her face with a length of
gauze. Her eyes were already swollen shut, ringed
by the distinctive ''raccoon eye'' blackening, a result of her fractured nose, and the rest of her face
was also beginning to swell. Such extensive facial
injuries were profoundly shocking to relatives because the patient was virtually unrecognizable.

Ben did his best to reassure her. ''I realize you

can't see, Gemma, and not being able to talk, either, is rough. This is painful and really scary, but I want you to know that you're gonna be just fine. We're taking you straight up to surgery. You'll feel better real soon.'' He gave quick instructions to the staff, arranging for a surgical team and an operating room, then he studied the X rays that had been taken.

He'd stabilize the fractured jaw immediately, and order CT scans. These would help him do a three-dimensional reconstruction of her bone structure before the accident, which he would use as a template for the major operation he'd perform to repair her face.

He'd schedule the operation within the next ten to fourteen days, before the fractures began to set. The delay would give the patient's system a chance to recover from the severe trauma of the accident and allow Ben to do the intricate computer imaging that was necessary.

That operation would be long and exacting; Gemma's facial bones were now like a huge broken-apart puzzle. But sophisticated technology and Ben's skill meant she'd almost certainly look the way she always had once healing was complete. That could take six months or longer.

There might be minor operations to remove scars after that, or some small adjustments to the original work, but nothing significant as long as the universe granted the two of them good luck and no nasty surprises in the next few hours, such as an infection that would result in a brain abscess.

Ben had no illusions or false modesty about his abilities; he was one of the best reconstructive surgeons in Vancouver. If Gemma was beautiful before her accident, she'd be beautiful again; it was just going to take time and painstaking effort. Already plotting strategy, he headed upstairs to the OR.

SERA CARDANO had finally bought a cell phone a week ago, but the sound of it ringing inside her handbag still caught her off guard. It was ringing now, and several moments passed before she realized what the sound was. Her mind was totally on the heated argument she and Maisie Jones, her boss and best friend, were having over the set for the next episode of the television sitcom *Dinah.*

Still determined that her choice of sofa over chaise longue for the love scene was the right one, she fumbled among the clutter in her bag and at last extracted the phone.

"Papa?" Just the way her father had said her name warned her that something wasn't right. "Papa, what's wrong?" Her heart gave a thump and then threatened to hammer its way through her chest wall, as her father's shocking words reverberated in her head.

Around her, the members of the design team gradually stopped talking. Everyone became ominously still, all eyes on Sera's horrified features.

"Honey, what is it?" Maisie hurried over to her and looped a plump arm around her shoulders.

"I've gotta go to the hospital. Right now." Hands shaking, Sera shoved the phone back in her purse, hardly able to speak. "It's my sister, Gemma. She's...she's had an accident. She was..." She gulped as the full impact of her father's words sank in. "Oh, my God, how could such a thing happen?"

How could it happen and she not know?

The room whirled around her and she worried that she was going to be sick or would pass out. "Gemma was hit in the face—a piece of lumber a forklift was moving. Her face is...she's badly hurt." Her voice seemed to come from a long distance away, and she barely heard the shocked gasps and exclamations of alarm that greeted her words.

"I'll drive. Which hospital?" Maisie grabbed her own purse and raincoat, then Sera's.

"St. Joe's, but I have my car. I can—"

"Not in this lifetime. You're in no shape to drive—you're in shock. And parking's a nightmare down there. I'll drop you. Don't argue."

Moments later, they were in Maisie's battered old Volvo, and as her friend skillfully negotiated the busy streets, Sera knew that Maisie was right. She wouldn't have been capable of driving. Her entire body was trembling uncontrollably, as over and over again her brain replayed the nightmarish image of her sister's face being smashed with a heavy piece of lumber.

"Now, don't get crazy until you know what the score is," Maisie admonished. "Things aren't usually as bad as we imagine. If she needs plastic surgery there'll be someone excellent to do it. Plastic surgery these days is a cinch. You remember I told you my sister's boy in Idaho was born with a cleft palate. They did such a good job you can't even tell…."

Sera barely heard Maisie's reassuring patter, but the sound of her voice was at least a distraction. When they reached the street in front of St. Joe's, Maisie nonchalantly stopped, blocking a lane of traffic. Horns blared and hands gave her the finger. Maisie ignored everything except Sera.

"I'll send good thoughts. You let me know if you need a ride home or anything at all. I'll leave my cell on. You do the same, okay?" Maisie leaned across and enveloped her in a bear hug, oblivious to the noise from the trapped cars behind them. "Good luck. I'm out of practice, but I'll pray."

"Thanks, Maise." Sera was out of the car and running for the entrance to the ER before Maisie pulled away.

BEN ROTATED his arms and tipped his head back to ease the knot between his shoulder blades. For two hours and forty minutes, his mind had been entirely consumed with the delicate surgery necessary to stabilize his patient, and now that it was done he was suddenly stiff and weary. Yet knowing that everything had gone as well as it possibly could have was exhilarating.

Without stopping to remove his operating-room garb, Ben headed out to the waiting room, where a nurse had told him Gemma's relatives had gathered.

The small room smelled of stale coffee, sweat and fear and was crammed full of people, standing, sitting, crouched in corners. If these were all Cardano relatives, Gemma had a big family. The ear-splitting clamor of voices subsided immediately when Ben entered.

Gemma's father hurried over, his arm around a plump, pretty middle-aged woman with a mass of graying curls. The strained expression on their faces told Ben how frightened they both were. He gave them a reassuring smile and reached out to shake their hands.

"I'm Dr. Ben Halsey."

"Aldo Cardano, and this is my wife, Maria. How is she? How's our Gemma?"

"She's doing well. She's in Recovery. You can see her in a few minutes. I've stabilized her fractured jaw and inserted a tracheal tube. I should warn

you she looks pretty battered. It'll be ten days to
two weeks before we can fully repair the facial
structure. I'm confident we can expect a good result
at that time. There shouldn't be any loss of vision.
The fractures didn't involve what we call the floor
of the orbit, the bones that support the eyeballs.
However, she might lose her sense of smell. We'll
just have to wait and hope that doesn't happen.
We'll be keeping a close eye on her, watching for
any signs of infection or excess swelling. But your
daughter's young and strong. Chances are she'll do
just fine.''

A buzz of relief and renewed concern circled the
room, and it seemed as if everyone drew in a deep
breath and exhaled it.

Aldo Cardano's soulful eyes filled with tears.
''Thank you, Dr. Halsey. Thank you very much.''

''This tra— This tube.'' Maria Cardano frowned
at Ben. ''Does that mean she can't breathe properly
on her own?''

''No. The tube's a precaution because she's unconscious and because she's had extensive damage
to her jaw. With the jaw wired, we don't want her
to choke.'' Ben smiled at the woman reassuringly,
thinking how attractive she was with her strong features and smooth, nearly unlined olive skin.

''Why do you have to wait so long before you
operate on her face? Why not do it right away?''
Maria wanted details.

"It'll be a long operation, and we want Gemma to recover from the trauma of the accident before we proceed. Also, I need to do some preliminary work first." Ben explained how he planned to rely on CT scans and computer technology to prepare for the surgery. Aldo appeared confused, but Maria nodded.

"Basically, I'll do a three-dimensional reconstruction of her uninjured face and then use it as a template."

"Like a pattern for how she looked before?" Maria shook her head. "But, doctor, you don't need a computer for that." Maria motioned with a hand. "Seraphina, come over here, *carissima*."

Mystified, Ben watched as a young, slender woman who'd been standing nearby and listening intently to their conversation moved over to Maria. She was obviously Maria and Aldo's daughter; she had her mother's bone structure and her father's long, straight nose and huge, deep-set brown eyes. Her golden-brown hair was long and loose. Untidy strands curled around her face; reflexively, she raised a hand and shoved them back.

She wasn't tall. Ben was five-eleven, and he guessed her about five-six, but her perfect posture gave the illusion of height.

"This is Gemma's sister, Sera." Maria spoke as if that solved the matter.

"Hello, Sera." Ben studied her. She had arresting good looks. "Your sister and you resemble each other?"

"Yes, we do," she said in a quiet, resonant voice. "Gemma and I are identical twins."

CHAPTER TWO

IDENTICAL TWINS? Having a living model for the extensive reconstructive procedure he'd be performing on Gemma Cardano was a stroke of amazing luck, Ben reflected. It would make the computer imaging much simpler.

This was a fascinating situation, one he'd never encountered before, one that intrigued him. He grinned at Sera, delighted. "That's fantastic, Ms. Cardano."

"Sera, please."

"Sera, then. An uninjured model to work from will simplify the process immensely. I'll need you to come to my office—if that's possible?"

She nodded.

"The office is right across the street from the hospital. Call my nurse and set up a convenient time. We'll take some photographs. They'll be helpful in the OR." His professional eye was gauging the curve of her cheekbone, the angle of her nose, the line of her jaw, and several moments passed before he realized his scrutiny was making her uncomfortable.

She met his gaze, but her color had heightened, and it dawned on Ben that Sera Cardano was a trifle shy.

"Sorry." He smiled at her and shifted his attention to the other people in the room. They were all silent, resolutely watching him and Sera, waiting for whatever else he had to tell them, and now it was his turn to be a bit uncomfortable. For a few moments he'd literally forgotten everyone except Sera Cardano.

"Mr. and Mrs. Cardano, the nurse will let you know when you can see your daughter. Swelling and discoloration are common in her type of injury. Also, there's always a fair amount of bleeding. So be prepared."

"How—how will she eat with her jaw wired shut?" Maria Cardano looked devastated. Ben surmised that food was important to her.

"We've inserted an enteric feed into Gemma's stomach—a tube that allows for continuous feeding. It's the easiest on the body for a while. It'll be there until we take out the trach tube."

"How long will she have to have her jaw wired?" Aldo's face was creased with worry, although he managed to keep his voice level.

"About six weeks. Once the trach tube comes out she'll be able to drink her meals."

Ben was trying his best to give them positive news along with the negative, but of course they were in shock as they faced the full extent of their daughter's injuries and the side effects.

"If you have any concerns at all, please phone me," he said when it seemed they had no other questions. "I'll give you my pager number." He reached for a pen, forgetting that he was still in scrubs.

Sera handed him a pen and a small pad of paper from the voluminous pockets of her denim overalls, and he scribbled down his number. He noticed that her fingernails were short and unpolished, her hands stained with something blue, and he wondered for an instant if she worked in construction like her sister. Then, amid a chorus of thanks, he left the room.

In the hallway, a tall, wiry man was leaning against the wall, head down, arms folded across his chest, broad shoulders slumped in dejection. He glanced up and straightened as Ben came by.

"Dr. Halsey? Doctor, how's Gemma?" His deep voice echoed with concern and apprehension. His rugged face was ashen beneath its tan, and his huge workman's hands were trembling. "My name's Jack Kilgallin. I—I was driving the forklift that hit her. The nurse over there said that maybe you would tell me how she is. I don't want to intrude on the family, but I really need to know how she's doing."

Ben recognized him as the man Leslie had

pointed out earlier by the phones. The poor bastard was obviously suffering the horrors of hell. Ben knew all too well how it felt to watch a friend come close to death because of an accident. Several years ago Greg Brulotte, Ben's best buddy, careered off a cliff while the two of them were skiing. Greg had recovered fully, but Ben still had nightmares where he stared helplessly into a deep ravine, knowing he had no way to get to Greg, feeling it would be his fault if Greg died. The memory haunted him, and made him want to reassure this man.

"She's in Recovery, Mr. Kilgallin. All we can do now is wait. The next twenty-four hours are crucial, but I believe she'll come through fine. She's a very strong young woman. The prognosis is good." Ben reached out a hand and squeezed the other man's shoulder. "Don't blame yourself, Mr. Kilgallin." His voice was gruff with compassion. "Accidents can happen to anybody."

Kilgallin's face contorted and he gulped. He was on the verge of tears. "I can't believe what took place. It was so fast. I looked away for one single minute—glanced over at the crane operator. Gemma just appeared out of nowhere. I should've seen her sooner. Damn, I'll never forgive myself."

"Hindsight's always a hundred percent."

"Will—will you be able to fix her face? She's— she's a real good-looking girl."

"I'll do my best. I promise you that. Similar procedures have had very positive results. I don't see any reason that shouldn't be the case with Gemma." Ben's beeper went off. It was his office number and he remembered that he'd forgotten to call Dana about rescheduling his afternoon appointments. She'd give him the sharp side of her tongue, and he deserved it.

He'd better get a move on; Dana wasn't the only one who hated keeping patients waiting. "I've gotta go. Don't be too hard on yourself, Mr. Kilgallin."

Kilgallin shrugged.

Ben hurried off down the corridor, forgetting about Kilgallin and thinking of Gemma and Sera Cardano, instead. He wondered how many times a surgeon had had a living replica of a patient to use as a model in reconstructive surgery. He couldn't remember reading about a single documented case history. Perhaps he'd write this one up for *JAMA,* the *Journal of the American Medical Association.*

He changed quickly and then rode the elevator down to street level and raced out the main exit doors. The rain had stopped, and Ben totally forgot the raincoat he'd abandoned hours before in the ER.

THE NURSE told the Cardanos that each visit should last just ten minutes, with a maximum of two people at a time. Sera's mother and father went in first. When they came out they both started weeping, their faces ashen.

"She...it's awful, Sera." Maria struggled for words. "She doesn't look like—like herself," she finally gasped, and Sera steeled herself as she headed into Intensive Care.

During the first few seconds the disturbing sights and sounds from other patients registered, but as she neared the bed where her unconscious sister lay, Sera was aware only of Gemma, and of her own heart pounding. She felt icy-cold and dizzy.

Gemma was propped up on pillows, and she was truly unrecognizable.

"Oh, God!" The exclamation was part prayer, part dismay. Her sister's face, always a mirror image of her own, was now grotesquely swollen and horribly misshapen. Blood oozed from her nostrils and the corners of her mouth. Her lips were almost invisible because of the swelling. Gemma's eye sockets were purple and blue, swollen shut. Her hair had been clipped close to her scalp on the right side of her head, where several strips of adhesive held the edges of a wound together. It, too, seeped blood.

A tracheotomy tube protruded from her throat; various intravenous lines extended from her arms and her stomach; electrodes on wires were attached to other parts of her body, carrying indecipherable beeps to a host of machines.

Sera gulped back a sob. What appeared to be ordinary wire cutters were taped to the end of the bed and an ominous-looking machine sat on the floor—shocking indications that things could go very wrong.

Most shocking of all, for Sera, was the utter still-ness of her sister's slender body beneath the crum-pled white sheet.

"Em?" Sera cleared her throat, unaware of using the contraction she'd formulated when the two of them were babies and she was too little to pro-nounce her sister's name correctly.

"Em, it's me," she whispered, wondering if sound could penetrate the stillness. Even if it did, where was Gemma?

Her sister was never this quiet, not even deep in sleep. Unlike Sera, Gemma was a restless sleeper, tossing, turning, muttering, thrashing her legs. At home they'd always shared a room, and Gemma had regularly fallen out of her twin bed, tumbling heavily to the floor and often not even waking up. Sera had never fallen out of bed, not even once.

Now, far more terrifying than the damage to her sister's face was this utter stillness.

"Em, are you in there?" Sera murmured the in-ane words and waited for some sign, but there was nothing. Gingerly she took her sister's fingers in hers, absently noting the roughness of Gemma's skin, the short, blunt-cut fingernails. They shared a total disregard for manicures; hands were tools, to be utilized to their fullest capacity. Sera's own fin-gers were still stained with the blue paint she'd used earlier that day on the set. Two of her fingernails were broken off painfully close to the cuticle, and she saw that Gemma, too, had several jagged nails.

A nurse appeared on the opposite side of the bed and briskly checked the IV and the monitors.

"What—" Sera had to clear her throat before she could force the rest of the words out. "What are the wire cutters for?"

"In case she vomits and starts to choke. So that we can cut the wires holding her jaw shut."

Lord. Sera shuddered. "And—and that thing?" She pointed to the device at the side of the bed.

"That's a suction machine. Again, in case she vomits or aspirates."

"Does—is that likely to happen?" *Gemma could choke to death.*

"It can, but we're watching her really closely."

"How come she's still bleeding like that?"

"With this type of injury, there's always a lot of bleeding. It's not excessive. Don't be too alarmed by it."

Easy for a nurse to say, hard to accept when the person bleeding was your sister.

"What's—what's the white stuff in that bag?" Sera gestured at the IV bag with the tube leading into Gemma's stomach.

"That's Isocal, a high-nutrient liquid formulated especially for patients who can't take nourishment by mouth."

"I see. She's sedated, right? That's why she's so quiet?"

"Yes, but there's a good possibility she can hear you, so talk to her."

For the next few moments Sera mouthed platitudes, assuring Gemma she was going to be fine, that she had the best plastic surgeon in the city, probably the entire country.

Sera didn't know that for sure, but Dr. Halsey had seemed reliable and trustworthy.

All Gemma needed to do, Sera went on, was rest and concentrate on getting well. By the time ten minutes were over, Sera felt like an undertrained competitor in a triathlon. Shaky and light-headed, she hurried out of Intensive Care, emotionally and physically drained.

One glimpse into the waiting room confirmed that even more of her relatives had arrived while she was away, and in typical Cardano style, they sounded as if they were talking at top volume, all at the same time.

Sera hurried past the door, around the corner and down the corridor toward the elevators. She felt as though she couldn't breathe. She needed fresh air, fast.

She punched the Down button on the elevator once and then again before becoming aware of the tall man she'd brushed past a moment earlier.

He was staring at her, his face ashen, and was

wearing soiled work clothes and heavy boots. Sweat stained each armpit.

"You've got to be Gemma's sister." His voice was deep and soft and rather gruff. "God, for a minute I almost... You look exactly like her. I knew she had a twin sister, but I didn't realize you looked so much alike."

"Who are you?" Sera was too exhausted even to be polite.

"Jack Kilgallin. I—I work for your dad." There was utter misery in his voice. "I'm the one who hit her, see. With the two-by-four. I was driving the forklift."

Sera remembered her dad explaining how the accident had happened and stating emphatically that it was no one's fault. This man obviously didn't share that view.

The elevator arrived and Sera stepped in, and then, on impulse, she touched the Hold button. Jack Kilgallin was already walking away, and the dejection in his slumped shoulders touched her.

"Mr. Kilgallin?"

He turned, and Sera said, "I'm going outside for some fresh air. You want to join me?"

He hesitated and then nodded. "Yeah, I do." He stepped into the elevator. "Thanks."

They didn't speak again until they were outside. Sera took a deep breath. Her chest ached, as if all the emotions she'd been controlling were trapped inside her heart.

"The rain's stopped." The brilliant sunshine hurt her eyes, but her sunglasses were in the handbag she'd abandoned upstairs in the waiting room. She drew in another deep lungful of air, tinged with fumes from the heavy traffic on Burrard but welcome all the same.

"There's a little garden this way, where it's quiet. Some of us eat our lunch there." Jack led her around a corner, along a narrow path between old stone walls. The path opened suddenly on an enclosed courtyard. Here the air smelled of freshly cut grass, and a stand of purple irises bordered a fountain and an old wooden bench.

"It *is* quiet." Sera sank onto the bench and tipped her head back, closing her eyes and letting the sun warm her skin. She realized she was cold, bone-deep cold, and she shivered and rubbed her arms.

She felt him sit down beside her, and she opened her eyes and looked at him. His elbows were propped on his knees, chin in his hands. He sighed deeply, and for a long while they sat in silence.

"The doctor thinks she's going to be okay, you know," Sera said after a time. "He seems pretty confident that he can repair her face so that she'll look the same as she always did."

"Yeah, I talked to him a while ago. He seems

like a nice guy." He drew in a breath. "You—you seen her yet?"

Sera nodded, and she couldn't restrain the shudder that ran through her. "A few minutes ago."

"How—how does she look?"

Sera swallowed hard. The mute appeal in his expression made her want to tell him it was better than it really was, but she opted for the truth. "Pretty awful. Hooked up to machines. Really still and out of it, but I guess they want her that way for a while."

"She'd hate that." His voice was thick, as if tears were close. "Gemma's like mercury, always moving."

It was an apt description, and Sera shot him a curious glance. "You know my sister? I mean, apart from work?"

He nodded. "Yeah. I took her out a couple of times."

Sera looked at him again, assessingly, taking in the gray liberally sprinkled through his thick, unruly black hair, his tall but muscular build, his huge, work-scarred hands. He appeared forty, forty-five even, an attractive man, solid, reliable.

He definitely wasn't Gemma's type, Sera thought. Her sister went for lean, hungry young men with fast cars and plenty of attitude.

He guessed exactly what Sera was thinking.

"She dumped me fast. Too old, not adventurous

enough.'' The faintest trace of a wry smile came and went, revealing even white teeth. He was truly handsome when he smiled. ''I wasn't going to take no for an answer, though. I intended to go on asking until she wore down.''

''You care for her.'' Sera felt even sorrier for him than she had before. He seemed a nice man, similar to dozens of other nice men who'd had their hearts broken by Gemma. She was good at it.

''Yeah, I care.'' His jaw clenched, and he fought back the tears that glistened in his gray eyes. ''I fell for her the first day she came to work with us. I'd do nearly anything for her.'' Raw emotion made the words ragged. ''Anything but hurt her. Or watch while she hurts herself.'' He swallowed back tears. ''I sure as hell never dreamed I'd do something like this to her.''

Sera tried to think of words to comfort him, but she came up empty. The events of the day had left her with little to offer anyone else.

''She never told me much about you,'' he was saying.

Sera nodded. It wasn't surprising that Gemma hadn't talked about her. Their relationship was complex and disturbing, and for a long time they hadn't been that close.

The truth was that for the past few years, Sera had done her best to distance herself from Gemma. Physically, they were identical. Temperamentally, they weren't. Her sister created turmoil, chaos, problems that Sera, more often than not, was expected to solve. Sera wanted peace in her life, and apparently the only way to have that was to sever the invisible cord that linked her to her sister.

"She said you didn't live here in Vancouver anymore."

"I don't, usually. Until two months ago, I was living in Los Angeles. I just moved back here temporarily because of a job."

And even here she'd been successful in distancing herself from her sister, Sera thought miserably. So very successful she hadn't even known when Gemma was in pain today, terribly injured, close to death.

It seemed to Sera that she'd managed, once and for all, to separate from the other half of herself.

But instead of triumph, all she felt was despair.

CHAPTER THREE

GUILT WASHED OVER Sera like stagnant, muddy water.

From the time they were babies, she'd always known when Gemma was hurt or scared, and Gemma had been the same. It was an unexplainable sixth sense that many twins had, even twins who'd been separated at birth.

When one of them had a major life crisis, the other knew on some level or even shared a similar situation. But today, there'd been nothing, no subtle change in emotion, no physical indication that might have warned her Gemma was hurting.

To think of her sister alone in such agony was unbearable. Unreasonable as it was, Sera felt she should have been able to somehow share it, make it half as painful.

"I should get back, find out if there's any change." She felt utterly weary, and she could see that same exhaustion in Kilgallin's eyes, in the way he moved as he, too, got to his feet.

"Look, Mr. Kilgallin, it's crazy to hang around here. Why don't you go on home and get some rest." Sera put a hand on his arm. "There's absolutely nothing any of us can do, and it'll be a while before she's allowed visitors except for family."

"Call me Jack, okay? And maybe I will go home. I'm sure not much use around here."

"None of us is. Give me your number, and I promise I'll call you and let you know if there's any change. Or better yet, you can call me." Sera rummaged in her pocket and found her pen and pad. Dr. Halsey's office number shared space with measurements from that morning's work on the set, which now seemed an eternity ago.

She ripped off a fresh sheet, scribbled her number and handed it to him. "You can reach me anytime. This is for my cell phone."

"Thanks." He reached for her pen, tore a minute scrap from the paper and scribbled his own number. "I'll be home in half an hour. I'll be in all evening. There's a machine if I go out for anything. If I can do anything for you or your family, anything at all, you'll let me know?"

Sera assured him she would.

Back in the hospital waiting room, she found that many of her relatives had now gone home, and it was a relief. Kind as everyone was, to deal with people just now was a strain.

Her mother and father were again in the Intensive Care unit with Gemma, and when they came out, Sera went in. There was no change in her sister;

she lay exactly the way she had when Sera first visited.

For the next hour, Sera and her mother and father took turns keeping a vigil at her sister's bedside.

Maisie called, as she had several times that day, and at six she arrived with two plastic carriers stuffed with food—bagels, cream cheese, soup, containers of salad, buns, cookies. Sera realized she hadn't eaten anything all day.

One of her father's brothers cooked in a restaurant, and he'd brought huge trays of pastries and antipasto, but she'd been too upset to eat. Now she was famished. The food tasted wonderful.

"How'd it go on the set?" Sera swallowed a mouthful of bagel and sipped from the container of soup as she and Maisie sat in the waiting room. She hadn't given her job a single thought all day. This was probably the first time since she'd been hired as assistant set designer for the popular sitcom that her work had been out of her conscious thoughts for so long.

She knew that she really shouldn't be away from it any longer than just this single day; they were filming in front of a live audience in three days' time, and Maisie needed her help for the dozens of last-minute tasks.

Maisie understood that Sera didn't want to hear reassuring platitudes or be asked endless questions about Gemma. She talked about work, instead, forcing Sera to think of something besides the Intensive Care unit.

"There's a big problem with the scene where Dinah and the Englishman go to the pub," she remarked. "The paint we used for the walls doesn't have enough depth. The cameras see it as flat. We tried using several different shades, but we couldn't get the tones to relate to one another in just the right way."

"I've got the model at home. I'll see if I can figure out what to do," Sera promised. "I should be at work in the morning. If something happens, though, and I have to be here, I'll call you."

Maisie gave her a reproachful look. "Don't be a martyr, okay? If you want to be here with your sister, be here. Don't even think of coming to work. I can bully everyone quite well by myself."

"Thanks, Maisie. I'll see how Gemma gets through the night."

They talked over other details relating to work, and Maisie left at eight-thirty. At nine Dr. Halsey came by again to check on Gemma. After examining her, he assured them things were going well; there'd been no extreme swelling or bleeding, no excessive increase in temperature. He was keeping Gemma sedated, and he urged the Cardanos to go home, promising that the staff would call immediately if there was any change during the night.

It was after midnight by the time Aldo and Maria

drove Sera to the deserted parking lot where she'd
left her car that morning. They reassured one another during the trip that Gemma was strong, that
she'd come through this fine, that she was blessed
to have Ben Halsey caring for her, that it was a
miracle things hadn't been worse.

Aldo insisted Sera spend the night with him and
Maria, but she explained that she would go to St.
Joe's early and then, if Gemma was okay, continue
on to work. Her parents' house was in Burnaby, a
Vancouver suburb, whereas the apartment Sera was
renting was closer to both the hospital and False
Creek, where the set was filmed. It made sense to
go home, but convincing Aldo took a lot of talking.

"Okay," he finally conceded with obvious reluctance. "But we'll follow you. Make sure you get
there safe and sound."

His authoritative manner irked Sera. She thought
of the years she'd spent in various cities far from
her father, but she gave in gracefully, sensing that
Aldo needed to feel that one of his two children, at
least, was safe this terrible night.

Outside her building's underground garage, Sera
stopped the car but left the motor idling while she
got out and ran over to give her father and mother
each a kiss and a fierce hug.

"I love you," she told them, seeing the strain of
the day etched in their faces.

She hadn't cried all day, but tears began to drip

down her cheeks as she pulled the car into her underground slot, and she was bawling in earnest as she rode the elevator up to the ninth floor. She fumbled with the key and lurched through the door into her dark, silent apartment.

She was crying for Gemma, for the pain and the disfigurement and the uncertain future her sister faced, but Sera knew she was also mourning a closeness that she and Gemma had shared as children and that was now gone. The accident, the unthinkable damage to Gemma's face, had reinforced for Sera the distance between herself and her sister; their physical likeness had powerfully linked them, whatever their differences. Now, however temporarily, it, too, was shattered.

She turned on lights and went into the small kitchen, blowing her nose on a paper towel. She mopped at her eyes, then heated a cup of water in the microwave and dunked an herbal tea bag in it. Leaning against the counter, she sipped the warm brew and thought about what it had been like to be born an identical twin.

Sera and Gemma had shared a womb, and until she was two or maybe three, Sera had believed that Gemma was part of her, instead of a separate person. What a shock to learn that her sister wasn't an extension of herself, like another arm or leg.

All during their childhood years, they'd been together. Maria had bundled them into the same large crib at first, and she'd often told the girls that when they were tiny babies, they'd sucked each other's thumbs as often as their own.

Later, their bedroom had had twin beds, but when they were little, they'd insisted the beds be close enough so they could hold hands during the night.

They'd grown up using each other's clothing, shoes, makeup and sometimes identity; they'd learned to tease relatives and friends who couldn't tell them apart.

But Sera had realized early, and painfully, that in certain ways she and her sister were very different.

At four, Gemma had stolen money from Maria's handbag for lollipops and told Maria it was Sera's idea. Both girls were spanked. Sera remembered to this day the feeling of unbelievable betrayal, knowing that Gemma had deliberately lied about her. It was Sera's first real recognition that her sister was capable of doing things she'd never do.

Maria soon caught on to Gemma's tricks, but when the girls started school, Sera more often than not bore the brunt of Gemma's escapades. Maria was an old-fashioned mother, with none of the savvy psychological insights that mothers of twins have nowadays. She delighted in dressing the girls alike, and it was easy for Gemma to insist that Sera was the guilty one when mischief happened in the classroom or on the playground. Because of her love for her sister, Sera always took the blame, but her heart hurt each time Gemma let her be punished for something she hadn't done. Sera could never have treated Gemma that way.

As teenagers, Gemma delighted in making a special play for any boy she knew Sera liked. Sera refused to compete. She hid her hurt and turned to art, something both girls had always been gifted at.

Gemma, always more physically active than Sera, went out for the track team and the cheerleading squad, and Sera began to appreciate and enjoy time spent away from her sister. She joined the drama club, and found she had little talent for acting, but she could envision exactly what was needed for the stage sets. She drew them, and her father taught her the basics of carpentry so she could build them.

In her senior year, Sera fell in love for the first time. Liam was an actor, not classically handsome or tall but funny and endearing and smart. He always seemed able to tell Gemma and Sera apart, and he seemed impervious to Gemma's bold sensuality.

Sera trusted him and gave him her heart, only to have it broken the night of the senior prom when she caught him kissing Gemma. Liam stammered that he thought it was Sera he was with, but it was a pathetic excuse; he'd never mistaken them before.

Gemma made a halfhearted attempt at apologizing afterward, but that was the moment Sera knew for certain she would have to make a life for herself, a life that didn't include Gemma. Her sister wasn't evil, but she was selfish, thoughtless, and manipulative.

And because of Liam, for a long time Sera was convinced that all men would eventually betray her. Sometimes she still wasn't sure she'd overcome that belief. She'd had several short-term relationships with men, but she certainly hadn't loved anyone enough to consider a long-term commitment.

Against her family's wishes, she'd left Vancouver after graduation. She and Gemma had both planned to attend university in Vancouver, but Sera had applied to and was accepted by the University of California in Los Angeles.

Gemma dropped out of university halfway through her first year. With Aldo's financial help, she started a boutique, but it was bankrupt in six months. After that, she went from job to job without finding anything that interested her for long.

She married at twenty-four, to a slick real-estate developer no one in the family could tolerate, and divorced fourteen months later, to everyone's relief. She continued going from one menial job to the next, until eventually she began working as a carpenter's helper for Aldo's construction company.

She'd stuck with it. The hard physical work suited her.

Sera remembered conversations with her mother in which Maria fretted over Gemma's doing construction work. "I know all this stuff about female equality, but it's too hard on a woman's body, and it's dangerous," she'd told Sera.

Her mother's concerns seemed prophetic now.

"Your father's told her a hundred times he'll send her to school to do accounting or business administration, but no, she refuses." Then Maria said what everyone in the family always said when there was a problem with Gemma.

"You talk to her, Sera. She'll listen to you."

And Sera had tried to convince Gemma to get training, she remembered now. She'd asked why Gemma didn't accept their father's offer, take up something less strenuous.

"I happen to like what I do," Gemma had insisted belligerently. "It's a no-brainer, it pays better than anything else I've tried and there're some spectacular bods on these macho construction guys."

There was no point thinking she should have been more insistent, Sera acknowledged with a sigh. If Gemma's mind was made up, nobody could change it. And neither could anyone change what had happened today.

Although the tea was calming, it was very late

and she was exhausted, Sera knew she wouldn't sleep. She had work to do on the set for morning, so she made her way into the bedroom, which she'd turned into her work area, outfitting it with a long table and the materials she needed for models. She slept on the pullout couch in the living room. It was a good thing there was no man in her life; making up a bed every night wasn't conducive to romance.

The light was blinking on her answering machine, and she pushed the button, then clamped a hand over her mouth when the first voice on the tape was Gemma's.

"Sera, it's me, I need to borrow that white silk suit of yours—you know, the one you wore to Valerie's wedding in April? Give me a call and maybe drop it off at my place in the morning. I need it for Saturday. Hot date."

Sera's face crumpled, and a sob caught in her throat. Weeks went by, sometimes a month, and she didn't hear from Gemma. There was something uncanny about the sound of that deep-throated eager voice now, when Gemma was lying in the hospital voiceless and unconscious, far from those who loved her.

The last thing Gemma would need for a while was a white silk suit, and the knowledge brought a new flood of tears.

But her sister was alive, Sera reminded herself, and that was the thing that mattered. They all realized only too well that she could easily have died today.

Dr. Duncan, the ER physician, had told them how fortunate it was that the accident had happened right on hospital grounds; transporting a patient with Gemma's injuries was always problematic, she'd said. And they were also fortunate, she'd added, to have a reconstructive surgeon of Dr. Halsey's caliber immediately available.

It took a few moments for Sera to pull herself together and concentrate on the work she had to do.

She reached for the scale model she'd designed to represent the pub scene. In the script the bar was owned by Louie, a regular character on the show, and Maisie had wanted the bar to reflect his doggedly glum personality.

The show was filmed rather than taped, which was good because nuances of shade were lost in taping, even though the technology had improved over the past five years. Contrast was still a problem, though. Maybe if she painted a subtly lighter shade on one wall, Sera decided, and then went two shades darker on the other, she'd achieve the desired effect.

She picked up her paints and began, and as the challenge of her work slowly forced her mind to focus, the gnawing worry about Gemma receded. Gradually, for the first time all day, she relaxed.

IN HIS SPACIOUS rooftop loft in Gastown, the oldest area in Vancouver and one of the latest to be gentrified, Ben smoothed his clay-covered fingers over the head of a child he'd just finished molding and then stood back to inspect his creation, nearly tripping over his dog, Grendel. The dog yelped a protest.

"If you'd move away from under my feet, this wouldn't happen," Ben reminded him as he patted an apology.

He smiled with satisfaction at his sculpture. It was the head of a full-cheeked three-year-old boy whose overwhelming curiosity and irrepressible exuberance were clearly evident in the wide grin, the raised eyebrows, the smiling eyes, the thatch of impossible hair that insisted on standing on end despite the efforts of the city's best children's stylist.

"Gotcha, Stanley Brulotte, you rascal." He peered at the photographs he'd been working from and, as always, felt a surge of affection for his outrageous little godson. Greg and Lily had produced a child who challenged them at every turn, taxed them to their limits and made everyone laugh.

Ben adored him, but limited his visits to two hours, max. The Brulotte household wasn't exactly geared to peace and tranquillity, and when Stanley's new sister or brother arrived in a couple of months, the situation could only get worse.

A glance at the old-fashioned alarm clock he kept

on the table surprised him. It was long after midnight, and he had a surgery at 7:00 A.M. Past time to clean up the clay, shower and head for bed.

He covered his creation carefully with a wet cloth and, after washing his hands, dialed the surgical ward to check once again on Gemma Cardano. He was relieved to hear that she was still doing well. It seemed that the universe was smiling on him, he concluded as he and his dog headed up the stairs.

If she made it through these first twenty-four hours without nasty complications, chances were good that the real danger was over. The reconstruction would be challenging, but certainly not life threatening.

He yawned and thought of his patient's sister, Sera Cardano. Twinning was a phenomenon that had always intrigued him, particularly from a medical standpoint. He'd recently read an article in a medical journal about identical twin males in their sixties who ended up in the same hospital on the same day with heart attacks and similar blockages of the coronary arteries. The chance of such a thing being coincidence was virtually nil.

How would it feel to have someone have the same life experiences as you at the same time, to have a constant reminder of how you looked, talked, laughed? Most people, he knew, had little or no true concept of how they appeared to others.

He could draw anyone, with uncanny accuracy,

from memory; it was a gift he'd had since childhood. But he'd have a difficult time drawing his own face without looking in a mirror, Ben mused. There was something about living inside a body that made it difficult to envision how that body looked to someone else's eyes…unless you were an identical twin.

Ben opened the window wide, checked the alarm and set the clock back on the packing case that doubled as a bedside table, idly reminding himself that he should do something about furniture. He'd lived here over a year now and the only area he'd bought anything for was the studio. Why couldn't he walk into a furniture store and purchase a couple roomfuls? Why did shopping always get put at the bottom of the list of things to attend to?

Because life held so many other intriguing things to do, and buying furniture was not his idea of a good time.

He climbed into bed and, after the usual tussle, Grendel settled on his dog mattress nearby. Every night without fail, the dog tried to climb in beside Ben.

Figuring himself out was hard enough, Ben decided with a yawn as he began to slide into sleep, without there being two of him.

The Cardano twins intrigued him, from a scientific standpoint, of course. Although he couldn't help but be aware that his patient's sister was an attractive woman.

Even a dedicated physician with a fondness for science wasn't immune to the power of testosterone, he told himself with a grin just before he slipped into sleep.

GEMMA STRUGGLED with every ounce of her will to wake up, to make sense of the buzzing voices, the monotonous sounds, that penetrated the void.

Wake up. She needed to wake up.

It must be night because she couldn't see.

Where was she? Low-grade anxiety came and went again.

''Can you hear me, Ms. Cardano? Gemma, can you hear me?''

The female voice, repeating itself endlessly, nagging, irritated her. She could hear. Why couldn't she see?

Terrible headache. Her face hurt.

Scraps of memory floated back, nightmarish recollections, of being strapped to a stretcher, of not being able to scream even though the pain was unbearable.

Panicked, she struggled harder to open her eyes. She couldn't.

Blind. She must be blind.

God, oh please God, not blind.

Gemma began to shudder, and whimpering

sounds came from her throat. They surprised her, because they didn't sound like noises she'd ever made before.

Something was terribly wrong with her throat. Something was very wrong, as well, with her jaw. It hurt in a way it had never hurt before, a monumental ache that made it impossible to lie still.

With a huge effort, she lifted a hand—and encountered a tube in her neck.

"Ms. Cardano, don't struggle, please. Your eyes are swollen shut. You'll be able to see once the swelling is gone. Your jaw was fractured and it's wired shut. You have a tube in your throat to make breathing easier. It's three in the morning, the day after your accident. Try to relax. Being relaxed is the fastest way to speed healing."

Eyes, jaw? God, what else?

She tried to ask, but the horrible croaking was all she could manage.

Thirsty, she was horribly thirsty, and her throat hurt like hell. She tried to raise her hand again, gesture at her neck, but her hand felt disconnected from the rest of her. It flopped back down on the sheet before she could make it do what she wanted.

The nurse guessed. "I know you must be thirsty, and I'm sorry, but I can't give you water just yet. We'll have to wait until we're sure you can swallow. You have a drip in your arm that's putting fluid into your body. I'm going to give you a shot now in your thigh. It'll help you rest. The more you rest the better. There's a call button right here…." Cool fingers took her hand and positioned it.

"Try to relax now, Ms. Cardano."

Rage flared. Who was this idiot telling her to relax? And she couldn't even holler that she hated needles. She tensed, waiting for the sickening instant when the needle penetrated her skin, but she barely felt it because the pain in her head, in her neck, was red and hot. After an interminable time it ebbed slightly and Gemma tried to concentrate, to remember the details of what had happened to her, but there was only a blur of separate moments with no connection between them. She clearly remembered driving to work in the early morning, cursing the rain because it was supposed to be summer.

Then there was a doctor, his deep voice soothing, telling her she was going to the operating room. And then the void came rushing up and swallowed her once more.

Darkness, and again a voice, one she recognized this time.

"Gemma? It's Mama, *carissima.*"

She had no memory of time passing, nothing to indicate where she'd been, only the darkness fading gradually as she became conscious again. She felt incredible relief, knowing her mama was beside her, holding her hand.

"Papa's here, too. It's six in the morning. He's just gone to talk to the nurse."

Gemma tensed, waiting for the sickening ache to start in her head, but it was duller. She felt nauseous, though, which was terrifying because she couldn't open her mouth. What would she do if she had to throw up? Panic shot through her, and she clutched at her mother's hand.

"They told us you woke up earlier," Mama was saying. "*Cara mia,* I should have stayed with you all night. I shouldn't have listened when they said go home."

It sounded like Mama was trying not to cry. Mama cried easily, so Gemma couldn't gauge the gravity of the situation from her. She'd know better when Papa came. She could always tell from the timbre of Papa's voice exactly how serious a thing was.

But it was Sera she really wanted. Sera could tell her the things Gemma needed answered, and she'd tell her the truth. One thing about Sera, she was big on truth.

Somehow Mama knew. "I called your sister. She should be here soon."

Staying awake was hard. The blackness ate her without warning, and again it seemed that no time elapsed before she heard a voice. Sera's voice.

"Em? Hi, Gemma. It's me."

Gemma moved her hand, blindly searching for

Sera's, and there was incredible comfort in the strength of her sister's cool, firm grasp.

"They're going to take your breathing tube out as soon as you're fully awake. Then it'll be easier for you."

Gemma tugged impatiently on Sera's hand. She needed to find out...

Sera understood. "I don't know how much you remember, Em. You got hit in the face...." Sera gulped and when she went on Gemma knew that it was pretty radical.

"You got hit in the face with a two-by-four. The bones in your face are smashed."

Her face was smashed? Gemma's heartbeat accelerated, and icy fear sluiced through her veins, but she tugged again on Sera's hand. She had to find out everything; had to.

"You'll be able to see as soon as the swelling goes down. Your eyes are fine. Your doctor's Ben Halsey. He's *il primo* as far as plastic surgeons go. He's going to fix everything as soon as you get stabilized. He's going to use me as a model, so you'll look exactly like me all over again unless you tell him you want some changes."

Gemma understood that Sera was trying to diminish the impact of what had happened. But she could tell just by the way Sera sounded that it was major.

"Personally, I'd hit him up for a shorter nose and smaller ears, Em."

They'd always joked about getting Papa's nose and Nonna's ears.

"We all feel pretty helpless. There doesn't seem a lot we can do to make this easier for you. Papa and Mama are staying here, but I have to go to work for a while—there's a problem with the set. I'll be back, probably by noon. It's seven-thirty now. I have to run. See you in a couple hours, Em."

Gemma felt Sera lift her hand, open the palm and press a kiss into it. "Bye, Gemma. Hang in there. I'll be back soon."

Gemma wanted to scream at Sera, tell her that she had no right to leave. Didn't she understand that Gemma *needed* her? But she couldn't talk and her entire head was hurting again, sharp and terrifying. She scrabbled desperately at the sheet, and suddenly her father's work-hardened hand enfolded her fingers.

"Be still, *principessa*. Papa's right here. I'll be right here beside you all day. You go to sleep now." She felt incredible comfort and reassurance in her father's presence, and with a sense of relief she allowed herself to slip back into oblivion and let time pass.

CHAPTER FOUR

FOUR DAYS HAD PASSED since the accident, and
Sera sat for the first time in Ben Halsey's office, in
a high-backed upholstered chair that looked beautiful but was decidedly uncomfortable. The seat was
too shallow and the back didn't adjust. The angle
was exactly wrong for any human spine.

She shifted from side to side, cursing whoever
had designed such a monstrosity, wondering ner-
vously just exactly what Halsey required of her.

She'd changed her clothes twice this morning before deciding on the straight-cut navy twill skirt and
the short-sleeved baby-blue vest over a white T-
shirt. Why she'd fuss over her clothes just to come
to see a doctor she couldn't explain. Normally she
threw on coveralls or jeans or walking shorts and a
shirt without any fuss at all.

"Ms. Cardano, good to see you." He smiled at
her, and she smiled back.

"Hello, Dr. Halsey."

He took the chair opposite, a match to the tor-
turous one she sat in. A small, scarred round table
stood between the chairs, instead of a desk. If that

was an attempt to make the office more like a living room, it failed miserably, Sera thought. The place could do with a coat of paint in a more cheerful color than this dull mushroom shade, and lordie, Halsey needed to spring for different chairs. He also could use a few big green plants to give the room more of a feeling of tranquillity, she concluded. The art on the walls was excellent, however.

She'd noted the unusual drawings immediately, charcoal sketches of almost grotesque faces that drew the eye and held it. Each stark drawing emphasized one feature, an unusual nose, or one ear larger than the other, or a dominant mouth. Only one sketch was more conventional, a free-form drawing of a small boy with impossible hair, devilish eyes and a rogue's grin.

Probably Halsey's son, Sera decided. Halsey wasn't wearing a wedding ring, but lots of people didn't these days. Or maybe he lived with someone.

"Gemma's coming along really well. I've scheduled her surgery for the twenty-third," he remarked.

Sera glanced over at the calendar on his wall. Today was the seventeenth.

"It can't be too soon. She's almost out of her mind about the way she looks." Even that was an understatement; Gemma had been so hysterical when she first saw her ravaged face she'd had to be sedated all over again, and since then, she'd alternated between bitter rage and depression.

"That's quite usual. She'll feel much more optimistic when the reconstruction is done and the swelling subsides enough for her to see that she looks normal again."

"She will, won't she?" Sera gave him an anxious glance. "Look normal again?" He'd assured them all that the chances were good that Gemma would look the same as she always had, but as each day passed, it became harder to believe. Her sister's face was shockingly disfigured, to the point where it made Sera nauseous to see her. Sera needed reassurance almost as desperately as her sister.

"Absolutely." He didn't even make his usual careful qualifications. Instead, he smiled, and she noticed how kind his smile was, and how it extended to his eyes. Behind his round, wire-rimmed glasses, those clear green eyes crinkled at the corners, filled with warmth.

She'd seen him numerous times in the past few days, coming or going from her sister's room. He'd always stopped and taken the time to fill Sera in on any changes in her sister's condition, even though she knew he'd already gone over every detail with her mother and father, and probably, as well, with the hordes of Cardano relatives who flowed in and out of the Intensive Care unit.

She'd seen him talking to Jack Kilgallin once or

twice, too. Jack was a constant visitor now that others were allowed in Gemma's room. He brought small bouquets of flowers, and tapes for the player Sera had transported in.

Her sister seemed barely to notice his presence, but Sera had concluded that Jack was a kind and considerate man.

Ben Halsey was also kind. The difference was, Sera found Halsey sexy, as well. She couldn't help but notice how attractive he was; no woman with breath in her body could miss it. He was deeply tanned, with an athlete's body, broad shouldered, not extraordinarily tall. Not an extra ounce of fat was visible beneath the checked short-sleeved shirt and tan slacks he was wearing today.

His dark-brown hair was beginning to turn prematurely gray at the temples, and although it was thick, he wore it cropped close to his well-shaped head. He had a strong, straight nose, and the round glasses emphasized beautiful green eyes and long dark lashes. His mouth was just full enough to be sensuous; his chin and jaw were strong and cleanly delineated; his teeth, white and even.

That he had wrinkles made his face interesting instead of just handsome. There were deep laugh lines at the corners of his eyes and mouth, horizontal creases on his forehead; it was obvious that in spite of his profession he hadn't had any nips or tucks himself. His face looked lived in.

"I like your drawings. Who did them?" Sera turned to inspect them again, using the movement to try to get comfortable. Didn't he realize these chairs were back breakers?

"I did, and thank you. Dana, my office nurse, was scandalized when I hung them. She thought patients would be put off by them, maybe conclude I was making light of their problems. Funnily enough, most patients don't seem to even notice."

"They're probably too busy thinking about what they want you to fix for them, and wondering how much it's going to cost and whether it will hurt." *And trying to get out of here fast to escape these damnable chairs.*

He laughed. "You're perceptive. Those are the exact issues that are raised in the first ten minutes of the first visit."

"Do you ever get tired of saying the same things all the time?" He made it easy to ask questions, even personal ones. In spite of his chairs, he made her feel comfortable, she supposed because he was so relaxed and easygoing himself.

"Nope, never. I love my work. It sounds sappy, but I consider it a great privilege to be able to help people feel better about themselves."

"I don't think that's sappy at all." She considered it noble, but she was too shy to tell him that. "Voluntarily having bits of me changed is not something I'd ever do. I guess that perfect or not, I like myself fine the way I am.''

Plastic surgery wasn't something she'd given a lot of thought to before Gemma's accident, but she'd seen enough actresses in L.A. change their appearance to know that plastic surgery was the norm these days.

''For people who aren't satisfied with how they look, I think it's great to have a choice,'' she went on. ''And for Gemma, of course it's essential.'' The idea of Gemma having to live with the face she had now didn't bear even thinking about. Sera shuddered. She was afraid her sister would commit suicide if there was no hope of repair.

''Thanks again.'' That affable smile came and went. ''And what about you? Do you enjoy your work, Ms. Cardano? What do you do?''

''Sera, please. With an *E,* because it's short for Seraphina.''

''Seraphina,'' he repeated slowly. ''That's unusual. I like it.''

She wrinkled her nose. ''I don't. It makes me feel as if I ought to be wearing a white robe and hauling a harp. Ms. Cardano, on the other hand, tells me I oughta be wearing a striped business suit and carrying a briefcase.''

He laughed. ''Okay, I'll settle for Sera. My name's Ben. So if you're not an angel, I gather you're not a lawyer, either—no striped suit or briefcase?'' He waited as if he had all the time in the world for her to answer his question.

''Nope, not a lawyer, although my dad would have been thrilled if I'd gone that route,'' she said. ''I'm a set designer, an assistant set designer at the moment, doing the set for a sitcom. And I'm the same as you—I absolutely love my work.''

He was obviously interested. ''Now, that's a fascinating job. You must have a lot of artistic ability. You have to draw the set first, don't you?''

''Yeah.'' Sera nodded. ''Then we build a model to scale. The trick is to make sure the set doesn't look like a set.''

''And it would have to take on the personality of the lead character, I imagine. If they were showing where the character lived, for instance?''

''That's right. Wow, not many people understand that.'' Sera was amazed and impressed by his immediate comprehension of some of the subtleties of her job.

''Do you always work here in Vancouver?''

''Nope, this is the first time I've been back to Vancouver on a job. I go wherever the work takes me. I worked in Chicago after graduation, doing stage sets, and then in Seattle for several years before I moved to L.A. I wanted to see if I could get into movies and television, which as you probably know do a lot of shooting in Vancouver. I was lucky to get this job, and it's such a bonus to work in my hometown.''

''Will you be here long?''

''For the next few months. Unless they decide to move the production somewhere else, which isn't unheard of.''

''Well, your being here is a stroke of luck, for your sister and for me.''

He stood up. ''If you'll come in here, we can begin.'' He opened the door to an adjoining room and Sera leaped up, grateful to leave the crippling chair behind.

She gestured at the drawing of the child as she passed it. ''Is this cute guy your son?''

''My godson. I'm not married, and have no kids of my own, for which I'm thankful each time I visit him. Stanley's what my mother used to call a 'holy terror.''' There were pride and affection in his tone. ''How about you, Sera? You married? Kids?''

''Nope, never been married. Gemma was for a short time, but I'm sort of married to my job, I guess.''

''I know what you mean.'' He gestured at a high stool. ''If you could sit up there, it'll make my life easier and your back sore, but I'll try to be quick.'' He turned on several lamps and aimed them at her face, doing his best not to shine them in her eyes.

''It can't be any worse than that chair in your outer office,'' she said without thinking.

What was she doing, making cracks like that? Gemma's face was in this man's hands, and here she was antagonizing him.

But he laughed instead of getting annoyed. "Those were gifts from my mother when I first opened my office. I've been planning on getting new ones, but I keep putting it off. Mom goes for form instead of function."

With a professional-looking camera, he snapped photos of her from every conceivable angle. As he did, he talked, a crazy stream of words that didn't require any response and were obviously intended to help her relax and take her mind off the fact that the stool was uncomfortable.

"I should have enrolled in a few classes in photography, but they never tell you that when you're a med student." He tilted her chin up with a gentle finger. "Perfect, that's perfect. Actually, it's amazing what they consider unimportant in a doctor's training. I guess everybody's heard by now about the two hours of nutritional instruction the average physician gets in training, but would you believe we never had even *one* hour's instruction in what the well-dressed physician should wear once he can afford to buy clothes? You'd think somebody from *GQ* would catch on that there's a lucrative potential market out there."

He moved to her other side, again tilting her chin

with a finger and rapidly snapping one photo after the other.

"They never even tested us for color blindness, can you believe that? What if a doctor ends up not recognizing blood because it looks gray to him? I'm not color blind, thank heavens, so I don't mix up blood and drool, or I don't wear purple shirts with yellow pants, but I don't have much clothes sense. I've got to rely on an outspoken office nurse who's quick to tell me which shirt doesn't go with whatever pants."

Sera couldn't help but giggle and he went right on snapping, coming in close, moving farther away. He was taking more photographs of her than she'd had taken in her life.

"I'm pretty lucky," he continued without a halt. "As I said, I've got Dana to clue me in if I go off track, but what about those poor devils just out of med school who don't have an office nurse to guide them? I suppose that's one of the reasons the majority of us marry in haste and repent at leisure." Abruptly, the flow of words stopped.

Sera had the definite feeling that he hadn't planned to reveal himself quite that much. He was silent for several long moments.

"Sorry," he said in a subdued voice. "I didn't mean to bore you with my personal history. My tongue works independently of my brain when I'm concentrating."

"Did you really marry just to get advice on your wardrobe?" Sera was teasing, but his answer was both shockingly straightforward and serious.

"I married because of hormones." His tone was rueful. "There was this incredible physical attraction." He set the camera down. "The problem is, sex is not always the best basis for a lasting relationship."

It certainly was appealing for the short-term, Sera mused. Having him so close to her activated her hormones, that was for sure. He smelled good, a clean woodsy scent. His breath was pleasant, natural, not masked by mint. This close to him she could see that his beautiful eyes had tiny flecks of gold mixed in with the green. He was a find, in Maisie's terminology.

"That's about what Gemma said after she divorced Raymond—that the big appeal was her ex's body, not his brain." Sera wondered if Halsey was a tiny bit chauvinistic in his attitudes. She challenged him on it.

He laughed. "Works both ways, of course," he conceded.

"Why did you decide to become a plastic surgeon, Ben?" Using his first name felt strange, but he *had* suggested it.

"Because of my great-grandfather. My father's family was from England. Great-grandpa Edward was a soldier in the First World War. He was trapped inside a bombed building in France in 1918, just before the war ended.'' He grabbed a straight-backed chair and sat down on it. ''He got burned. Face mostly. Hands, too. Body not as bad. He was sent to Queens Hospital at Sidcup in Kent. The doctors there were experimenting with grafts and other early techniques for restoring facial features, and they did what they could for him.''

''That's awful. Was he married?'' She considered what it would be like for a woman to marry a handsome young soldier and have him come back terribly disfigured. It would take an unusual person.

''Nope. He married after the war. I never knew my great-grandma—she was dead by the time I was born. But apparently she was a really special lady.''

''Were you born in England?''

He shook his head.

''Edward and his new wife immigrated to Canada in 1923, to a farm in Saskatchewan. My grandfather was born there. He grew up and married the girl on the next farm. They had six kids. Dad was the youngest. Mom was a schoolteacher he met in Saskatoon. I never really thought anything about Great-grandpa's face being different until we were visiting the farm one summer and a kid I was playing with said he looked like a monster. I beat the stuffing out of the guy.'' His smile was satisfied.

''And that's when you decided to become a plastic surgeon?'' It was such a romantic story.

"Nope. I wanted to be a soldier, like Great-grandpa. I was fascinated by guns when I was little."

She had to laugh at the incongruity.

"But before he died, Great-grandpa talked to me about the war, and the doctors he'd known in Sidcup, who'd devoted their lives to helping men with injuries to their faces and hands, doing their best to send them back into the world looking better." This was clearly a subject dear to his heart.

"You know, the unofficial father of plastic surgery was a guy named Kazanjian. He was really an American dentist. He went over to France with the Royal Army Medical Corps, and with raw skill and inventiveness earned himself a name as The Miracle Man of the Western Front. Grandpa told me stories about Kazanjian—he'd actually met the guy. During my teens, I didn't even think of being a doctor, but when I got to university, I decided on medicine."

He stood abruptly, as if he'd finally remembered he had other patients to see. "We're all done here. Now I'll send you over to St. Joe's for a CT scan. You've been really patient, thank you."

She arched her aching back. "You're dead right about that stool. It's pretty bad. Not quite the back breaker those chairs are, but close."

He laughed. "So, Ms. Set Designer, what would you suggest, instead?"

"A bar stool in here, very padded, with a back-rest that adjusts. And for out there, a couple of wonderful leather chairs that you sink into and don't want to ever get out of."

"And where would I find those?" He seemed perplexed.

She shot him a scandalized look. "You're joking. The city's full of furniture places."

He shook his head. "I'm totally serious. I'm absolutely at a loss when it comes to shopping for anything but groceries."

"You simply go to a furniture store. In fact, I'm sure I saw the perfect leather chairs last week when I was hunting down a sofa for the set."

"I wish I'd known. I would have had you buy them for me."

She still couldn't believe he was serious.

"I'm going back tomorrow for a footstool. Do you want me to watch for some chairs?"

"Would you?" He looked as if she'd offered him her body. Or maybe he wouldn't be quite this enthused over her body.

"Sure." Shopping was such an easy thing, one she enjoyed doing. "I'll find you some, and a stool, as well. I'll tell the salesperson you'll be in to check them over."

He appeared alarmed and shook his head. "I'll never do it. Just pick them out, call here for my credit-card number and have them delivered. I'll tell Dana. She'll handle any other details.''

Sera was astounded. ''Furniture's expensive. You really oughta see it before you invest money.''

''I trust your judgment. I never know what to get or where to find it.'' His grin was rueful. ''You know, I moved into a new place over a year ago and I still haven't furnished it.''

''Want some help with that, too?'' The words were out before Sera could stop them, and she was immediately horrified at her audacity. But turning living spaces into reflections of the people who occupied them was irresistible to her. If she wasn't doing set design, she'd be an interior decorator. ''S-sorry, that was presumptuous of me,'' she stammered. ''I—''

He interrupted. ''You mean it? Because if you do, you bet I want help,'' he said fervently. ''How soon could you stop by? Could you come this evening and maybe have a look?''

Sera began to wonder what she'd gotten herself into.

''Yes, I guess I could,'' she finally said. ''Sure. After I visit Gemma.'' What the heck was she doing?

''Fantastic.'' He sounded delighted. ''About, what, eight-thirty, nine? Here's my address. It's a loft in Gastown.'' He scribbled on a pad, ripped the sheet off and gave it to her. "Any suggestions at all would be much appreciated.

AFTER SERA LEFT, Ben stood for several long moments, thinking about what had just occurred. Until today, he'd seen Sera only as Gemma's attractive twin, a fortuitous aid to his patient's favorable reconstruction. But in the past half hour, she'd become an individual to him, a singular woman with a fascinating job, self-confidence, a sense of humor; all the attributes he most admired. And that she was pleasing to look at didn't hurt, either.

He was drawn to her, no doubt about that, which was why he'd so readily accepted her offer of assistance with his office chairs and his loft. He didn't really give a damn about the loft, but he did want to get to know Sera outside his work environment.

She was unconventionally lovely. She had that mass of wild curly hair the color of polished oak. Her ears and mouth were a shade large, her nose a trifle too long to qualify for traditional beauty, but that was exactly what appealed to him so strongly.

That and the fact that Sera Cardano had quite casually stated that she was comfortable with her looks, satisfied with them. To Ben that was both unique and astonishing.

Certainly not all, but a high percentage of the women he dated sooner or later made it clear they wanted something changed—smaller noses, bigger breasts, higher cheekbones, thinner thighs. Not that he accommodated them; he usually referred them to a colleague if they were absolutely determined to have surgery. Reluctantly he'd come to accept that part of his appeal was the knowledge that he could, if he chose, play Svengali.

Quite simply, his job intrigued women with the promise of physical beauty. And although he wasn't proud of it, in his early years he'd sometimes taken advantage of that fascination with plastic surgery to promote a relationship.

The fact was, he truly liked women; he had a brother but no sisters, and females had always been both mysterious and exciting to him.

For several years, Ben and Greg Brulotte had nurtured a reputation as St. Joe's most eligible bachelors, driving fast cars and dating wild women. Since Greg's marriage four years ago, Ben had sorely missed having a buddy.

He'd gradually changed, living a quieter life, devoting more time to his art, although he'd still managed to meet and date plenty of women. He'd thoroughly enjoyed several intimate relationships; indeed, the last one had ended just two months ago when Monica Halko had decided to move to Toronto.

She was the editor of a small Vancouver magazine, and she'd been offered a job at a much larger

publication in Toronto. She'd halfheartedly suggested Ben accompany her, but of course that
wasn't part of his career plan, and she understood
that. They'd parted amiably enough; they'd talked
on the phone, although not in the past several
weeks.

Ben suspected Monica had found another companion, which bothered him not at all. He'd probably meet the guy somewhere along the line; a lot
of his romantic relationships eventually evolved
into casual friendships.

The single notable exception was Vera, the nurse
he'd married at twenty-four and divorced a scant
year later. He didn't like to think about her. He'd
hurt her deeply, and he felt profoundly guilty for
what had happened between them. As he'd blurted
out to Sera, their union had been based more on
lust than on love, and he hadn't realized until later
that Vera was mentally unstable.

He'd vowed after his divorce never to hurt a
woman again, and to the best of his ability, he'd
upheld that vow. He made absolutely certain the
ladies he dated understood from the beginning that
he wasn't looking for any sort of long-term commitment. He'd gone out of his way to tell them that
he didn't get involved in serious relationships. He
was interested in a good time, and the women he
dated understood that.

"Dr. Halsey, are you all right? Mr. Tate's been

waiting for over twenty minutes.'' Dana's voice was reproachful.

"At once, *sir*.'' Ben snapped her a salute, and she laughed and shook her head at him.

He was nearly always good-natured, but that afternoon he found more reasons than usual to smile and laugh and tease. He knew it was because he was very much looking forward to seeing Sera that evening.

CHAPTER FIVE

SERA WALKED PAST his building twice before she finally found the nerve to press the buzzer beside Ben Halsey's name.

He lived on the top floor. The elevator was slow, and all the way up she wondered what exactly she thought she was doing. It wasn't characteristic of her to come on to guys. Did Ben feel that was what her impetuous suggestion had meant? She felt embarrassed now, wondering how to deal with the situation.

He was waiting when she stepped out, and his wide smile welcomed her.

"Sera, glad you found me okay." He led her a short distance down the hall. He'd changed into worn jeans and a white T-shirt. His feet were bare, and that relaxed her somewhat; it made him seem vulnerable, not so much a doctor. He'd left his door open, and now he stood aside so she could go in ahead of him.

A big brown dog came trotting over to her, wagging his tail and sniffing her pant leg.

"This is Grendel. He's friendly and harmless. Useless as a watchdog, but great as a companion."

Sera loved dogs. She hunched down and let the dog sniff her and lick her cheek. "Hiya, fellow."

Grendel woofed and offered a paw. Sera took it and the dog made happy whining noises.

"That's it. Now he's in love. He's a pushover for the ladies," Ben pronounced. "He's not gonna let you move anymore without him underfoot."

"We'll manage, won't we, boy?" Sera scratched behind Grendel's ears and got to her feet, looking around. "Wow, is this ever big." It was a penthouse loft, with huge skylights set in a cathedral ceiling. There was a compact, well-equipped kitchen to the left of the entrance. On the right was open storage area, with a racing bike hung on a hook and an enormous heap of sports paraphernalia on the floor.

Intrigued, Sera walked farther, into a huge living room that ended in a dramatic wall of glass stretching from the bare plank flooring almost up to the ceiling two stories overhead. It gave a panoramic and breathtaking view of the harbor, the North Shore mountains and the busy streets of Gastown far below. The day had been hot and sunny, and even though it was late in the evening, light still streamed in through the window and trickled down from the skylights.

"Oh, I love this. I envy you this space. What a

fantastic place to live. I'm renting a furnished apartment with a view, but it's nothing like this."

"Thanks. I really like it here." It was obvious her sincere praise pleased him.

At one end of the cavernous room, Ben had set up a table for sculpting and drawing. A long piece of plywood held clay and a canvas-wrapped work-in-progress. An easel sat beside it, with oils and charcoals scattered on the floor and table.

"This is spectacular, all this space," she breathed, turning slowly in a circle, her eyes following the floating staircase up to the loft.

Each time she moved, Grendel moved with her, gazing up at her with limpid brown eyes.

"I'm really glad you approve," Ben said. "I just don't know how to furnish it."

"The possibilities are endless."

He laughed. "Not to me they're not. Before you get into explaining, how about a drink? I have wine, soda, orange juice. Or I can make coffee or tea."

"I'd love a glass of wine."

"So would I." He headed into the kitchen, and she patted the dog and watched as Ben opened a cupboard, found stemmed glasses, took a dark bottle from the fridge and poured chilled white wine.

"Sit down."

Glancing around again, Sera realized her choices were limited: one of four bar stools fronting the half wall that opened to the kitchen, or either of two plastic lawn chairs set up before a large television.

Sera chose a lawn chair, and Ben followed her lead, sinking into the other one. Grendel plopped down in the space between, his head on Sera's feet, his tail thumping irregularly on Ben's.

"Cheers." Ben lifted his glass to her. "How was Gemma this evening?"

Like a crazy person, Sera wanted to say. Her sister had thrown things, cried, torn up notes before anyone could read them. "She's pretty scared about the operation," she finally said, realizing now that was the real reason for Gemma's tantrums.

"She's afraid you won't be able to make her look the way she did. Afraid of being scarred and disfigured, of having people stare at her and feel sorry for her. She hates not being able to talk, having to write everything down." Being able to verbalize the things she instinctively knew were bothering her sister helped. It dispelled some of the irritation and utter frustration that Gemma's behavior caused.

The wine helped, as well. It was cool and tart, smooth and refreshing.

"Gemma always cared more than I did about how she looked," Sera reflected. "She's used to getting a lot of male attention."

Ben nodded. He listened well, and that was comforting. "As I told you, there aren't any guarantees, but I think Gemma will be pleased when I'm done.

In the meantime, of course, it's really tough for her, and being in the hospital doesn't make it any easier. She'll feel better when she goes home.''

''When will that be?'' Gemma had an apartment of her own, but she'd agreed to stay with their parents until she'd fully recovered. Sera felt a stab of sympathy for her mom and dad; her sister wouldn't be an easy patient.

''Within a couple days of the operation, providing all goes as planned.'' He smiled at her again, a relaxed, warm smile that put her at ease.

''So what's it like being an identical twin, Sera?''

She took a few moments to reply; it was a question that had no easy answer. Usually, the person asking wasn't interested in an in-depth response, but she sensed that Ben really wanted to know.

''I guess it's like everything else in life, part good and part not so good,'' she finally said. ''You're never really alone, since even when you're not physically together, there's this deep sense of connection. But you miss being an individual, too. Not now so much, because I moved away, detached myself, but when we were kids everyone thought of us as one unit, sort of GemmaandSera. And that was hard, because we *are* separate people, with a lot of differences.''

He nodded. ''I understand.'' He paused a few seconds and then added, ''When I first met you,

I'm afraid I was guilty of exactly that—thinking of you only in conjunction with Gemma—since having a living model to work from was convenient for me. But I don't think that way anymore, Sera.'' He was quiet for a long moment, looking at her, and something in his scrutiny this time made her fully and uncomfortably aware that he was an attractive man and they were alone together.

Flustered, she searched for a neutral topic.

''You said you've lived here a year. Where were you before that?''

''Oh, in Vancouver. This city's my home. I doubt I'll ever leave. A friend and I had bought a beach-front house as an investment as well as a place to live, but then he got married. So I sold him my share of it and moved into a furnished suite for a while. This area was just starting to develop. I happened to know one of the owners of this building, and I got first choice in apartments. Wanna see upstairs?''

''Yes, please.''

He and Grendel led the way up the spiral staircase to the loft. There was a king-size bed, neatly covered in a brown-and-green-striped duvet. Beside it was a packing case that served as a bedside table. Grendel made his way over to a plump brown doggy mattress next to the bed and flopped onto it. Here, as downstairs, no rugs covered the plank flooring, and there were no closets, either.

Ben had suspended two long rods from the ceiling and hung his clothing on it. He used a stack of pullout baskets in a steel frame as drawers. The only real furniture was an elaborate sound system on an oak stand, a matching CD holder, filled with disks, and a makeshift brick-and-board bookshelf.

"You like music."

"Can't live without it."

"Me, either."

She examined the books he'd left strewn on the bedside table. "You like mysteries?"

"English ones, yeah. What do you read for fun?"

"Stephen King."

"Hey—me, too," he admitted. "And poetry. I read a lot of poetry. It's relaxing."

"We took it in school, but I haven't ever thought of reading poetry to relax." He'd surprised her again.

"You play a lot of sports, Ben?" She remembered the pile of equipment downstairs.

"My work's pretty sedentary. I need to get out and do physical stuff in my off time."

"What sports do you most enjoy?" She was very aware of being alone with him in his bedroom.

"Oh, biking, swimming, skiing. Soccer. I'd like to coach a kid's soccer team if I could ever find the time. And fishing. I love to fly-fish. Again, I don't get much time to do it."

Sera moved to the area of the loft that had been partitioned off to form a large and lovely bathroom. It had an enclosed shower and an immense oval tub, elevated and facing the window that formed one wall of the room. He'd stapled a blue-striped sheet to a pole to serve as a window covering.

"Practical," she remarked, not trying to hide her amusement.

"Well, I didn't want the entire waterfront watching me have a bath."

"Of course not." She fantasized for a guilty delicious moment about him in a bathtub.

Get a grip, Sera.

She glanced at him. He was eyeing her, and again she felt a prickly sort of awareness between them.

"Shall we go back downstairs? I think I've seen enough up here to have a feeling for what needs to be done."

He stood aside so she could lead the way. Grendel also politely waited for her to go ahead.

"This staircase is really effective. I can see it being used on a set. Staircases are great props. Actors love them because they can make grand entrances and exits."

She was babbling. She stopped herself and took a deep breath as she reached the bottom of the stairs. "How the heck did you end up without any furniture if you shared a house?"

"The house was furnished by a decorator. Several decorators. I never liked the stuff very much—lots of flowered couches and tiny tables and beds with tops on them. It suited the house, so I gave my share of it to Greg and Lily as part of their wedding gift. They're the parents of Stanley, the kid in the drawing you admired at the office.'' He got up and went over to the worktable. ''I'm doing him in clay now. Then I'm going to cast the piece in bronze and give it to them for Christmas. Come and see what you think.''

Sera went over to the table as he carefully removed the coverings on the clay sculpture, revealing the image of a boy so real and vibrant it made her smile and exclaim softly in admiration. ''It's alive, Ben. Oh, it's marvelous. You're very talented.'' She reached out a tentative hand and stroked the boy's hair, which stood up in wild clumps.

''Did you ever think of becoming a sculptor instead of a doctor?''

''For one insane moment when I was sixteen, yeah. But my mother very wisely arranged for me to meet a well-known artist, a carver, and he told me how long it took him to begin to eke out a bare living. He didn't try to discourage me, just told me the facts, and I decided it would make a great hobby. I knew even then that I didn't have the dedication to spend years doing something that might or might not earn me a decent living.'' He shot her a deprecating grin. "There's this greedy side of me. I like good transportation and nice restaurants. So I sold out."

He was looking at her again with that focus that was becoming familiar. Maybe it was just the way he looked at everyone. Maybe it was because he was an artist. Maybe it had nothing to do with attraction. She hoped she was wrong.

"I'm impressed all to hell that you've made a career out of your ability as an artist, Sera. I know it's not an easy thing to do."

"If it hadn't been for my father, I'd probably have given up and gotten a job as a receptionist or something after I left university. But Papa always made certain I had money and a credit card and a decent place to live, so I was able to volunteer for theater projects, and that gave me valuable experience that came in handy when I applied for paying jobs. I was lucky, too. In L.A. a set designer for one of the major television studios took me on as an apprentice. Her name's Maisie Jones—I'm now her assistant designer. It's a big thrill to get paid good money for what I was happy to do free." She'd also gained a friend in Maisie, which seemed an incredible bonus.

She was talking an awful lot.

"You're talented. They're lucky to get you." He had such honest admiration in his voice that she flushed and shrugged.

"I tell myself that to keep my confidence up. The truth is, I have some ability, but there are lots of people around with far more talent who never succeed. A lot of it's being in the right place at the right time."

And meeting someone like Maisie Jones.

"Luck." He sounded thoughtful now. "I guess plain old luck has a lot to do with success, all right." He smiled at her again, and the seriousness was gone.

"I figure meeting you was lucky, Sera. I might otherwise have gone on living without furniture for the rest of my life. That is, if you think you can steer me toward what this place needs."

"I'm sure I can make suggestions. You just have to decide whether it's what you want." Something puzzled her. "How come you didn't just hire a decorator, the way you and your friend did with the house?"

He shook his head. "Oh, we didn't hire Belinda. She was a, um, sort of a close personal friend."

A lover. Sera speculated about how many women there were in Ben's past. A long line of them, she'd guess.

"Anyhow, she offered to do the house for us. Greg was the same as me—not a clue when it came to decorating. But she nearly drove us both to suicide. Fabric samples, carpet samples, paint colors, this kind of look, that kind of look." He actually shuddered. "By the time she was half done, she and I weren't speaking and Greg wouldn't come home if she was there. She finally quit on us, with everything in such a mess we had to do something. So we hired this other decorator. Really tall, middle-aged, very solid, a big lady, maybe 350 pounds." He shook his head, and the horrified expression on his face made Sera laugh outright.

"She was far worse. She changed the color of the living room three times, she had a carpenter knock out walls, she turned us out of our bedrooms for weeks. We fired her eventually. Drew straws to see which of us had to do it—we were both scared as hell of her—and I lost. Anyhow, we were in an even worse mess than the first time. The next person we got was better, but the process was still like having surgery without anesthetic, in my opinion. I wouldn't ever get myself into that situation again."

Sera was still giggling. "What makes you think I won't be the same?"

"You won't be, will you—because you're not an interior decorator?" There was a hopeful, insanely plaintive note in his voice. Sera loved it. Ben was a genuinely nice guy. *And sexy as hell with those jeans and big bare feet. Don't go thinking this is something it isn't,* she cautioned herself sternly. *This guy is a mover when it comes to women, way out of your league, more Gemma's type.*

And a broken heart wasn't exactly high on her

list of priorities. Not that she'd had one since high school; she'd never ventured that far again.

But he wasn't breaking her heart at the moment; he was making her laugh, instead. He was doing everything he could to amuse her, to take her mind off Gemma, and she appreciated it. There hadn't been a whole lot to laugh about since the accident.

BEN LOVED the way her smile lit up her whole face. There'd been that amazing electricity upstairs when they'd mutually recognized each other's sensuality. He'd savored the moment, but he sensed that afterward she was a little on edge, and he wanted her to unwind, to enjoy the evening as much as he was. He'd been so right about her; she was enchanting.

"Okay, Ms. Cardano, tell me what you think needs doing here. Don't hold back. I'm a big strong guy. I can handle it. But first—" he reached for her wineglass and refilled it along with his own "—a little anesthetic to dull the pain." He took a hearty slug, grimacing as if it were medicine. "Better, much better. Now I'm ready."

She was grinning at him, her brown eyes twinkling.

"First of all, paint. The size of this place, gallons and gallons of paint."

"Oh, curses, I knew you'd say that." He clutched his heart and feigned cardiac arrest. "Paint, my worst nightmare."

She pretended to ignore his antics. "A deep, sultry taupe is what it needs, I think. There's all this light pouring in. We need to soften it a little. And the ceiling gets done, as well, two shades darker than the walls. Unless you have an aversion to taupe?"

He frowned at her, still playing it up. "What is taupe exactly? I've been at cocktail parties with taupe, but I swear we've never been introduced."

He wondered if she had a man in her life and concluded there had to be one around somewhere. When she relaxed like this and laughed and waved those expressive hands around, she was irresistible.

"You know what taupe is. Stop teasing. This is serious business. Your entire reputation is at stake. A man is judged by his environment, and it has to be the right color. Now, on this window you need roman blinds, which roll up and down, again to control the light. In an abstract print, brown and white and green. And some industrial wall sconces along here—" she gestured "—just at eye level. On this wall, closest to the kitchen, a huge mirror, to reflect and make the best use of the softer light you'll get with the walls painted. It'll also reflect the mountains."

She might have been speaking a foreign language. And anyway, he was watching the way her mouth looked instead of listening.

"That's it? That's all? Well, hey, that's not as

bad as I anticipated. No worse than a root canal.''
He heaved a gigantic sigh of mock relief and took
another drink of his wine. ''Come sit down in my
living room and take a break now that the painful
part is over. I'll put some music on and we can rest.
What kind of music do you like?''

''Almost anything except jazz.''

''Country-and-western okay? Grendel prefers
it.'' Ben chose a Willy Nelson CD and turned the
volume to low. He flopped into a lawn chair beside
her.

''Brace yourself. We're not quite done yet,'' she
said firmly once they were settled.

He groaned and tipped his head back.

''I'd paint everything but the bathrooms the same
color, then use a blue-gray on them for contrast.''
She was enjoying this. It showed in her voice. ''Oh,
and in the upstairs bathroom you need some of
those vertical blinds, the kind that allow you to see
out without anyone being able to see in.''

''Now, there's a unique concept. I could use
some of those in the OR when the gallery's full and
things aren't going as planned.''

She shook her head at his nonsense. ''In your
bedroom, two big armoires would work well as
closets, and a couple of antique trunks could store
linen and towels. And a big old dresser would be
nice. Oh, and rugs. This place is screaming for

huge, colorful dhurrie rugs on these rough wood floors.''

"I must be going deaf. I've never heard even a murmur.''

"You just don't speak the language.'' She grinned at him, that impish grin that he wanted to see again.

"Neither do I have a clue where to begin to get the stuff you've just talked about.'' He hoped she'd fall into the trap he was setting. "I don't even know a wall painter—they mustn't be big on nose jobs.'' He gave her a supplicating look. "Do you have time to do this for me? Not the painting, just the supervising and stuff. Making the decisions. I'd pay you, of course. Just decide on a fee. *Any* fee, within reason, as long as I don't have to be involved in what's going on. And I wouldn't have to move out while it's happening, would I?''

"Of course not. It would probably help if you could stay out a lot for a day or two while the painters are working, but it's not essential.''

"So you think maybe you could mastermind this transformation for me?''

She hesitated, and he realized that he really wanted to see more of her. He absolutely didn't care about the apartment. His mother had offered more than once to do something about it, but he knew she tended toward fragile furniture and pastel colors, so he'd managed to put her off. It truly wasn't a problem for him to live this way; he liked the starkness and he suspected Grendel did, as well. But if Sera agreed, it meant he'd get to know her better, and that appealed to him.

It was also easier than immediately asking her out on a date, he reasoned. He'd have to give her his dating manifesto if he did that, explain that he was looking for a good time and nothing more, and he had a gut feeling that might not work with her.

"As long as you're not in any hurry, I guess I could probably do it," she finally said. "Somedays I have to work on the set till late, but on others I'm done early. What sort of budget are we talking about?"

"Certainly not more than this place cost me," he stipulated, tongue in cheek. "And you've guessed I'm not into collecting antiques or making the sort of decorating statement here that would get me interviewed by what's-her-name...Martha Stewart."

"I can't believe you even know who Martha Stewart is."

"My mother's a big fan of hers. She has her books and watches her shows on television."

Sera nodded but didn't comment. "Well, I'm used to doing sets that appear spectacular without my spending much money. This sitcom is the first thing I've worked on that actually has a decent budget."

"How about if I give you a figure and then whatever you don't spend is yours? Let's see. That decorator we had cost us…'' He did a silent accounting and then named an amount that he felt was acceptable.

Her face mirrored her astonishment, and she burst out laughing. "Ben, that's ridiculous. I could redecorate my mother's entire house for that.''

He shrugged. "This might cost more than you think. Why not go with that figure and we'll negotiate later?''

She gave him a look. "Okay, if you insist. This is exciting. You rich guys really think big.''

It was his turn to laugh. "I knew this luxurious loft would give you the wrong impression. I cannot tell a lie, Ms. Cardano. I hate to admit it, but I'm not rich. To make really big money I'd have to move to Beverly Hills and get myself some high-profile clients, excuse the pun. And that's not my idea of a good time.''

"What *do* you want to do?'' She was serious, and he thought about how long it had been since anyone had asked that and hoped for an honest answer.

"Exactly what I'm doing.'' But even that wasn't the whole truth, and he needed to be honest with her. It was suddenly easy to tell her his dreams. "I'd love to head up the new burn unit at St. Joe's.''

"That's part of the construction work my dad's company is doing, isn't it?"

"Yeah. I can't wait to see it finished and in operation. The treatment of burn wounds has always been of great interest to me."

"Because of your grandfather."

"Yeah, and because of the challenge it represents. I worked in India once, treating burn victims. I'd like to do more of it."

"Well, if you want it that much, you'll get the job." There was absolute conviction in her tone. "Obviously, you have the qualifications, and you have a great reputation. Everyone at the hospital's told us how lucky we are that you're treating Gemma."

He was deeply touched by her ingenuous faith in him.

The reality was that not everyone thought that way.

Ben was all too aware of a powerful enemy who'd do everything to block Ben from getting the sessional appointment he so wanted. Ben's former wife, Vera, had an uncle on the hospital's administrative board. Dr. Roderick Miller made no secret of the fact that he despised Ben Halsey.

Ben had no idea how much influence Miller had with the other voting members, but he did know for certain Miller wouldn't be voting for him to head up the burn unit.

He could do nothing about it, so he did what he always did when there was no solution. He put the problem firmly out of his mind and concentrated on the pleasure of the moment.

"Tell me more about your job, Sera. How does a television sitcom get produced? Are you in on it from the beginning, or do you just look at a finished script and draw the sets?"

"I wish." She grimaced.

He liked to hear her speak. She had a distinctive way of pronouncing her words that was pleasing and that likely stemmed from her Italian heritage.

"Set design begins with the creator of the story line," she continued, "and after that it becomes a team effort, with the director as boss. We're really lucky because the director of *Dinah* is great to work with. Then—" she paused dramatically and ticked off her fingers as she spoke "—there's a co-producer, an assistant director, a second assistant director, a dialogue coach, a script supervisor, a technical coordinator, an art director, the director of photography, the camera crews, the carpenters, the painters, the electricians."

"Whew."

"Right." She nodded and shoved her thick hair behind her ear. "As I think I said before, I work with Maisie Jones. She's an incredible art decorator who's done lots of sets for television."

"Tell me more," he urged, genuinely intrigued. "What's the main concern for a set designer?"

"What's called the look of the show. We want to give the illusion that the viewer is seeing real life, so details are really important. And you always have to remember the cameras, the angles they'll be shooting from, the lighting." The animation in her face and voice when she talked about her job delighted him.

"So it's not just being able to come up with the right chair or sofa, then." He knew it wasn't. He wanted her to go on talking.

"Nope, although that's important." She was suddenly shy. "You could come and visit the set sometime, if you wanted. I'd be glad to show you around."

"You would? I'd really like that, thank you." He was touched by the offer, and sincerely interested. "I'll arrange for a few hours off soon, as long as nobody would get upset. Is there much temperament to deal with among the actors?"

"Not that I've seen, not on this set anyhow. There was more when I worked in theater. Television actors as a rule seem to focus more on the job and less on their egos."

"I know a few doctors whose egos get in the way of their work. From what you describe, surgery and sitcoms have a lot in common. Team effort, cooperation, dedication to a fine result."

The full moon was shining in the window. Ben hadn't turned on any light except for the one in the kitchen, and the semidarkness and good conversation contributed to the sense of intimacy between Sera and him.

She was enchanting in the moonlight. She had a subtle air of whimsy and unspoken promise about her created by the mass of wildly curling hair, the almost lyrical way she moved her unadorned hands to make a point, the generous spirit that came across so clearly in her conversation.

He'd like to take her to bed. He'd *love* to take her to bed.

The languid music curled around them, and Ben had the sense, rare in his experience, that this particular moment in time was as good as it got, bed or not.

He was disappointed when she glanced at her watch and made a horrified sound in her throat.

"My gosh, is *that* the time? I've gotta go. I have to be on the set at six-thirty tomorrow. And you probably have surgery or something. I've kept you up." She got up and started looking around for her handbag.

Grendel woke up and staggered to his feet.

"Surgery, yeah. Keeping me up, no. I don't go to bed early." Ben ached to say. *Can't you stay? Will you stay?* But of course he couldn't ask that; he hardly knew her. He wanted her badly, though.

"But don't you have to do, well, sort of homework, for the operations?" she was asking. "Work them out ahead of time?"

Her bag was just inside the kitchen, on the floor. He handed it to her, and Grendel gave a sad little whine.

Ben knew exactly how he felt. "Depends what it is. Tomorrow will be the third operation on a gentleman who had cardiac surgery some time ago, a quadruple bypass. He got infection repeatedly around the incision, and by the time I saw him, it had spread to the sternum. We had to cut away skin, remove diseased bone, use the abdominus rectus muscle—"

He stopped abruptly when she shuddered. "Damn. I tend to forget not everybody's fascinated by the removal and repair of body parts."

"Oh, but I am, Ben. Who wouldn't be? It's just that..." Her face colored and she looked abashed. "Well, I guess I assumed you did mostly face-lifts or tummy tucks or nose jobs, that sort of thing. I mean, I know you're Gemma's doctor, but I just never thought much about what other surgery you do."

He laughed. "Plenty of elective stuff, of course, but I also have a lot of patients like Gemma who need reconstruction, either from accidents or disease. The variety appeals to me." He winked at her.

"If you really are interested, I'll go into vivid detail for you next time. I could do slides."

"Maybe I'll skip the slides." She moved to the door, where she turned to look at him. "Thanks, Ben. I really had fun. And it was an honor to meet you, Grendel." She bent to give the dog a farewell hug.

"Damn dog gets all the perks." He took a step toward her and then couldn't resist reaching out and coaxing her into his arms. He touched her curly hair, brushing it back from her face. It had looked wiry, but instead it was silky to the touch. She was almost the same height as him; he had maybe an inch on her.

He leaned toward her, hoping against hope that she wouldn't draw away.

She didn't, so he kissed her, careful to keep it light, a getting-to-know-you sort of kiss, tasting, testing, gentle.

She didn't throw herself into his arms the way he half wished and didn't expect, but she didn't pull away, either. The kiss lasted longer than he'd dared hope for, and her full lips were sweet and voluptuous and, after a moment, eager. He felt like groaning with relief. He pulled her closer, slid his arms around her waist and fitted their bodies together, and the kiss deepened, intensified. His heartbeat followed suit.

He felt himself grow rock hard, wanting her.

She couldn't help but feel it. She drew back, her eyes startled, her expression vulnerable. He caressed her swollen lips with the ball of his thumb.

"I really do have to go now, Ben." There was the slightest tremor in her voice.

"Wait a moment. I'll get my shoes and Grendel's leash and we'll walk you to your car." He couldn't remember where the hell he'd left his shoes, to say nothing of the leash. He couldn't remember much of anything except how kissing her had felt.

"Oh, you don't have to come down with me. That's not necessary." She was flustered.

"But it is. My mother taught me a gentleman always sees a lady to her pumpkin." He located his shoes in the pile of sports gear. Now, where in hell had he abandoned the leash?

"Grendel, leash." And Grendel, smart dog that he was, unearthed it in a corner of the kitchen and came trotting over with it. "Humor us here, okay? We're doing hero training."

Ben pulled on the trainers, tied the laces, snapped the dog's leash in place and took her hand in his, threading his fingers through hers. Her skin was a little rough, and she had calluses on her palm. He lifted her hand to his mouth and kissed it, pleased when she shivered.

In the elevator, he surprised himself by saying, "Is there someone special in your life, Sera?"

"As in, do I have a lover?"

He liked that about her, her directness.

"Yeah."

She shook her head. "I don't seem to be marvelous at the man-woman thing. I do Hello, Nice to know you, Goodbye." She gave him a challenging look. "What about you?"

"I'm alone." He stared straight into her eyes. "Only for a couple months recently. But what I had with her is over. Truth is, I'm not much good at long-term, either." He hesitated, wondering why he felt compelled to tell her again. "I was married once, a long time ago. I was a terrible husband."

She just nodded.

He wanted to ask her if she'd take a chance on short-term with him, but he decided not to. They'd do the decorating thing and see where it led.

He was aware of the way she drew a little closer to him when they reached the noisy street. A loud argument was taking place between three men who'd had way too much to drink. He liked feeling as though she wanted him to protect her.

Grendel growled, and the men moved a few steps away.

Her car was small, white, not new, messy, filled with sketchbooks and bits of carpet and other stuff he couldn't identify. He held the door for her, and waited until she'd turned the corner at the light before he and the dog walked slowly back toward his building.

CHAPTER SIX

"HEY, GEMMA, how're ya doin'?"

Visiting hours were almost over for the day.
Gemma was sitting in the only comfortable chair in
the room, a worn armchair. Being up made her
woozy.

She turned slowly toward Jack Kilgallin and list-
lessly waggled her fingers.

Not being able to talk was awful. Not the worst
part of all this by far, but bad enough. Her mother
had just left, and Gemma was exhausted. Maria insisted on being cheerful no matter how bitchy
Gemma got. She hated herself for being nasty to
her mother, but the pain was making her crazy.

She was counting the minutes until the nurse arrived with her medication. Her head ached; her
neck was on fire from the tracheotomy tube. Dr.
Ben had decided it should stay in until after the
reconstruction; apparently her nose would have to
be packed, and with her jaw wired breathing could
be a problem. Having to live with the trach was just
one more major irritation in a series that were becoming increasingly hard to tolerate.

She longed for the drowsiness of the drug, for the numbness it brought. She *wanted* to be drugged, lost in lala land so she didn't have to feel. She'd let the nurse administer the shot and then she'd close her eyes and welcome the oblivion of drugged sleep.

Whatever they gave her was a little like smoking grass but way more powerful. She wished Jack wasn't such a tight-ass; she'd ask him to bring her some grass instead of those flowers and magazines and CDs and stuff; she could probably inhale it through the lousy tube in her throat.

But she knew better than to even ask. Jack didn't do grass, or much of anything else except the odd beer. She'd found that out when she'd dated him.

She'd invited him to take her to a party where things were happening, and he'd refused point-blank.

"That crowd'll get you into big trouble, Gemma." He'd sounded like her *father,* for cripes sakes. Yet for one nanosecond, it had felt so good to have Jack taking care of her.

He'd been right about her friends. They weren't exactly loyal; she'd found that out in here. They'd come to visit her exactly once, right after the accident, and she'd had the awful feeling it was for the kick of seeing how bad she looked.

But then, what could she expect? She wasn't exactly the life of the party anymore. Would she ever be again? The constant fear surged inside her, making the blood pound in her ears.

"It's really hot out there, even this late in the evening," Jack was saying. "I guess summer's finally here."

He put the new magazines on the bedside table and set the jar clumsily stuffed with tulips and freesia on the windowsill. He always brought something.

"How you feelin', Gemma?" He reached for the pad of paper and pencil she used to communicate and handed them to her.

Suicidal. Sick to death over this whole mess. Mad as hell that it happened to me. Bored and sore and fed up and scared shitless. But she didn't write any of that down; she couldn't reveal herself that openly to him. Instead, she just scrawled a careless *Okay* and tossed the pen aside. The poor bastard felt bad enough without her twisting the knife.

She wished he'd just give it a rest, though. This coming by every spare minute, dashing up at his lunch break, stopping by again in the evening like this. It was plain as anything that Kilgallin was eaten up with guilt. He needed to get a life.

Still, to give him credit, he'd apologized only once, the first day she was conscious enough to understand what was going on. He'd cried then, which had shocked her silly. Big, tough Jack Kilgallin in tears?

Since then, he hadn't had much to say. But he'd never really been the verbal type. She'd gone out with him only twice, and it seemed a long time ago now. He hadn't had a lot to say then, either.

The thing she remembered about dating Jack was the raw physical attraction between them. She hadn't slept with him, no credit to her; he'd stopped before things had gone that far. She would have slept with him, though; they'd nearly devoured each other once they'd started kissing. The chemistry had been astounding. But he wasn't a party man, and that had ended it for her.

She still liked him, however, in spite of his outdated attitudes. So when he'd apologized about the accident, she'd scribbled a note telling him that what had happened was nobody's fault, that she didn't blame him, although for the first week or so that was a total lie.

She *did* blame. She blamed her father for hiring her on the crew in the first place; she blamed the hospital for wanting a new unit built; she blamed herself for being in the wrong place at the wrong time; she blamed Jack for not paying more attention to what the hell he was doing. She blamed everybody.

When she'd come out of the blackness enough to fully understand what a total mess her face was, she'd wanted to die. She'd wanted to curse, shout, scream, but of course none of those was an option;

the sounds she made with her jaw wired and this tube in her throat were disgusting, subhuman.

At least they matched the way she looked.

The only time the blackness eased a little was when Dr. Halsey was around. He was the sole person who really understood how she felt, Gemma decided. Everybody else went on about how glad she should be that she'd survived the accident, how well she was coming along, how much better she looked; didn't they have eyes in their heads?

She was a monster, and she knew it.

The first time Gemma got hold of a mirror she truly wished she'd died in the accident; she'd rather be dead than spend the rest of her life with that for a face. Nobody except Sera would talk about how she looked. Good old Sera was honest to a fault.

"It's pretty much a mess, Em," she'd admitted when Gemma had pressed her for a comment. "But it won't always be this way. Doc Halsey's gonna fix it. It's strictly temporary. You've gotta keep that thought in your head every minute. Six weeks from now I'll bet you won't even know you'd ever been in an accident."

Those assurances were scant comfort when they came from Sera; her sister wasn't exactly a medical genius.

But coming from Dr. Ben, they actually made Gemma feel a little better. She'd asked if she could call him Dr. Ben, and he'd laughed and said of course, she could call him whatever felt right.

She liked and trusted him, and for some weird reason she didn't even mind him looking at her; there was something about his matter-of-fact manner that convinced her he saw beyond the devastation of her face. He made her feel safe; he gave her hope; he wasn't fazed one tiny bit by her mask of Frankenstein. He'd seen it all before, and he understood. More than that, he cared.

"It's tough to have to go through this, Gemma," he told her. "But you have to think of your injuries as lasting only a few months out of a long lifetime. Just endure. You're going to be pretty again. I guarantee it."

He'd grinned at her and given her a roguish wink, and for one instant she'd felt like her old self again, attractive, flirtatious, able to charm any man she wanted.

"Because you and Sera are identical twins, I can do the repair ideally, so trust me on this, okay?" And then he'd explained in detail, with sketches, exactly how he was planning to give her back her face. She couldn't believe him at first when he said he and his colleagues could do the whole thing in one long operation. Or that there'd be no incision.

"The surgery is done through the palate and the nose." He'd shown her the original X rays and the

CT scan, which indicated exactly where and how the bones were broken.

"We've already repaired your jaw. That's one big job already completed." He showed her on the scan where the breaks had been, then pointed to her cheekbones, nose. Even she could see scattered bits of fractured bone. "I'll just put all this back together like a puzzle. With computer imaging, I know exactly where the pieces should go, and as I've said, having your sister as a model helps immensely. It'll take six weeks or more before the swelling and bruising go down, but right after the operation you'll start to look like yourself. Just keep staring at your sister and telling yourself that's the face you'll have again, the intriguing face Sera and Gemma Cardano share."

She'd asked him if he'd sign a promissory note saying that she'd come out okay, and he'd laughed. She'd smiled, too. He was the only one who could make her feel like smiling these days.

As much as she trusted him, now that the operation was only a day away, she was petrified. Any sane person would be at the thought of eight hours, maybe even more, under anesthetic, with no real guarantees except Ben's word that she'd come out human in appearance, never mind the way she used to be. Just as Dr. Ben said, Sera was her lifeline; it wasn't what her sister said or did these days that helped. It was simply that by looking at Sera, Gemma knew how she ought to look.

She'd been in hospital only eight days, but it felt like an eternity. She'd had a lot of time to think, and she'd reluctantly admitted to herself that she hadn't been blameless in what had happened to her; out late the night before, she was hungover when she'd come to work that fateful morning.

She could remember the throbbing headache, the nausea in her belly, the feeling of being in a fog that morning.

Accepting blame didn't stop the bitterness and anger that welled up inside her, though. Sure, she'd been careless, but the extent of the punishment for that second of carelessness was out of all proportion. Instead of thanking God for her life, which Mama and Papa went on and on about, Gemma hated God for doing this to her. She was furious with Him, and she didn't hesitate to tell Him so, but as usual, He didn't pay any attention to her griping.

So more often than not these days, she transferred that feeling of frustration and pent-up rage to Jack Kilgallin, just because he was around so frequently. It irritated her beyond measure that he didn't fight back. Trying to see how far she could go before he lost his temper and walked out on her was a challenge. Afterward, she felt rotten, ashamed of herself. Maybe she acted the way she did with him because of the bitter knowledge that whatever passion had existed between them was gone for good. Who could look at her now and want to do anything other than vomit?

Who could see her now and, even if the operation worked, be with her in the future without remembering her like this? She didn't want to be with anyone who had memories of her looking so bad.

Jack picked up a fashion magazine and held it up. "You want me to read to you, Gemma?"

He'd done that when her eyes were still too swollen to focus, reading newspaper articles and magazines. He read well, which surprised her. Reading out loud wasn't an easy thing to do. Some of her teachers at school had driven her nuts, they were so bad at it. She'd enjoyed having Jack read to her.

Tonight, though, she refused. Today had been harder than usual to get through. A group of medical students had come by that morning, some of them young and male and attractive. She'd been asleep, and just for a split second as she awoke, she'd forgotten what she looked like. She'd assessed them the way she used to do men; which one would she flirt with first?

And then, like an anvil crashing down, she'd recognized the expression in their eyes, the impassive gazes that classified her as an unfortunate woman with a destroyed face. They didn't know that only a few short weeks ago, she could have chosen any of them, and with her smile and her smart mouth and a certain provocative glance she'd perfected in adolescence, she'd have had them at her beck and call.

Tonight she hated what she'd become, and instead of anger, tears were close.

"Did you get a chance to play that new CD? Want me to put it on for you now?"

She couldn't even shake her head. She snatched up the pen and the pad. *Get the hell out. Leave me alone.*

"Sure, if that's what you want." Even-tempered as always, he headed for the door just as the nurse arrived to give her her medication. "See you tomorrow, Gemma. You need anything, just have the nurses let me know," he said just before the door sighed shut behind him.

"That's a great guy you've got there," the perky nurse commented in such a cheerful tone Gemma wanted to smack her. "He's good-looking, too. Tell me where you caught him and I'll go fishing in the same place."

With the nurse's help, Gemma climbed stiffly up onto the bed and lay back on the pillows carefully, so carefully; her head and neck were agony. Clumsily, aware of the trach tube in her throat, she turned on her side, making it easy for the nurse to give her the shot.

She felt the prick of the needle, the ache as the medication began to diffuse through her muscle.

She wanted to tell the nurse Kilgallin wasn't hers; he was available. The nurse could do her best to attract him if she wanted.

Self-pity and weariness overwhelmed Gemma as the drug began to do its job. The last clear thought before oblivion claimed her was rebellious. She didn't want any man who stuck around her just out of pity, the way Jack was doing.

What was the old saying?

She wouldn't want to belong to any club in which she was a member.

CHAPTER SEVEN

"SO HOW does she look?" Maisie Jones leaned across the table and squinted at Sera. "I guess it's too soon to really tell—she's bound to be swollen—but d'ya think the operation was a success?"

Yesterday's reconstruction of Gemma's features had taken twelve and a half hours, and Sera had been absolutely terrified for her sister. Being under anesthetic that long had to be dangerous, plus there'd been the terrible uncertainty about the outcome.

"It's hard to believe, but you can already tell that she's going to look like herself again. She can go home in a couple days. The swelling and bruising are pretty bad, but it's obvious that when she heals she'll look the way she always has. Like me."

"He's gotta be a genius, your Dr. Halsey." Maisie gave Sera a sly glance. "So now let me get this straight, luv." She tipped her mug of beer and took a hearty swig, her cornflower-blue eyes dancing with mischief.

"You picked out chairs for his office and you're decorating the hunky doctor's loft out of the good-

ness of your generous heart, in your spare time—"
she rolled her eyes and blew a raspberry "—which
everybody knows we don't have any of in this job,
to say nothing of visiting your sister and having
dinner three times a week with one of your gazillion
aunts. But you don't have any fantasies, you claim,
about taking him to bed in his *loverly* newly refur-
bished bedroom?" She snorted again and took another drink. "What d'ya think, I've spent the past
ten years masquerading as a vestal virgin?"

Sera laughed. The idea of rowdy, outspoken
Maisie as a vestal virgin stretched her imagination
to its limit. She was glad the little pub where they
were having dinner wasn't full of people, so they
could talk in relative privacy. Not that Maisie cared;
she was prone to saying whatever was on her mind
at the very moment it came to her, in a voice that
carried.

"I haven't done anything about his loft yet except check some paint samples. And I didn't exactly
say I don't have fantasies about him." She felt her
skin grow hot and wouldn't look at her friend.
She'd had more dreams, waking *and* sleeping,
about Ben Halsey in the past week than she cared
to admit. "Any female between eighteen and eighty
would. I said that I wasn't sure I wanted to get
involved with him."

"Going to bed is pretty involved, honey."
Maisie could and did switch from teasing to dead

serious in a heartbeat. "Unless you're one of those people whose heart and lower extremities aren't on the same circuit, having sex is playing with matches. Sex for the sake of sex—that's a testosterone game guys pretend to play. It's not about affection or love—it's about power. And it backfires on them as often as not." She narrowed her eyes at Sera. "I was a teenage kid back in the free-love hippie days in the Haight in San Francisco, don't forget. I gave the polygamous approach a damned fair try." She shook her auburn head, and feathery strands of hair floated and settled again around her pretty, heart-shaped face. "Didn't work for me. I fell in love with the director who was making out with me and the lead actress and the understudy, and it broke my heart. This was before the big AIDS crisis, of course. I was liberated. I did the same as he did, went to bed with whoever was available. It was what you did at that time. God, it's a wonder we didn't all die of venereal disease, never mind a broken heart."

She leaned over the table, her lavish breasts spilling out of the low neck of her flowing dress. She spoke slowly and clearly. "It was the loneliest I've ever been in my life. And I learned a hard lesson about myself. I'm monogamous by nature. Granted, it's been serial monogamy—three marriages and a couple affairs along the way—but never more than one relationship at a time, and that one with somebody I cared for deeply. While it lasted. Unfortunately things change. *I* change.'' She frowned. ''Now I've lost my place. Where were we before I got on the subject of my misspent youth?'' She dipped her spoon into her bowl of maple walnut ice cream and slowly licked it, her plump face screwed into a grimace of ecstasy as she followed the ice cream with a sip of beer. ''Man, this is living.''

''How can you eat ice cream and chase it down with beer?'' Sera was drinking bottled water. Beer gave her a hangover, and ice cream a headache. ''The chocolate cake's good, though. For a pub, this place has great food.'' She was making an effort to get Maisie off the subject of Ben.

It didn't work.

''Just don't get your heart broken, okay, luv? The rumor mill has it that your hunk of a doctor is nothing if not fickle when it comes to women. He deals in multiples, one after the other after the other. Serial monogamy, like me, but way out of my league when it comes to sheer quantity.''

Now why, Sera wondered, did she instantly feel alarmed and defensive? She hid her reaction and kept her voice light. ''He pretty much told me that. He said he'd been married, and that he wasn't good at it. He said he'd had a relationship until a couple months ago. He's honest, which is all you can ask. And who the heck have you been talking to about him anyway?''

What if it got back to Ben that somebody from the television crew was asking personal questions? She'd be humiliated. He'd naturally think it was her.

"That local guy who's working with Irby on lighting, Kenny what's-his-name? Well, he has a sister who's a radiologist at St. Joe's."

"And she used to date Ben? She *is* dating Ben? She's planning on dating Ben?" Sera tried to keep her voice steady. There was a peculiar tightness in her belly.

"Nope. She's fifty something and married. She just told Kenny what apparently is common knowledge at the hospital."

"*Maisie.* You *asked* Kenny to find out about Ben." Sera shot her friend a reproachful look.

"Well, better to have all the facts. Or fiction, depending on how accurate hospital gossip is." Maisie reached across the table and took Sera's hand, and her voice softened.

"The word on the street is, Dr. Halsey's a love-'em-and-leave-'em guy, and I just don't want you getting hurt, okay? Having sex with the Ben Halseys of this world is like playing with nitroglycerin. It's spectacular if you're prepared for the explosion, but I'm not sure you are."

Her beautiful eyes were kind and concerned. "I've known you, what? Two years now, two and a half? And in all that time you've never really fallen for anyone, never even shown a whole lot of interest in the entire male gene pool when it comes down to it. And some of the guys who were hot for you were to die for. You do attract men, in case you didn't know it. Probably because you're such a challenge.'' She cocked her head and studied Sera. ''Maybe it's that wild hair combined with the dose of cool attitude. That camera guy with the ponytail, for instance. Now he was a *specimen*.''

''Jeff. Yeah, he was nice.'' She'd dated him half a dozen times. It had been nice. Comfortable. No sense of drowning, no blood pooling in her abdomen, no urge to tear off her clothes and let herself slide down his body to the floor the way she'd felt the night Ben kissed her. Just remembering that kiss brought goose bumps out on her arms.

''You don't have to worry about me, Maisie. I'm twenty-eight. I've been around enough to be able to take care of myself. Besides, neither Ben nor I is interested in a scenario that includes a cozy house and a nanny.'' Too late, she realized she'd revealed more than she'd intended to.

Maisie gave a satisfied grin. ''So you talked over the pros and cons, huh? Now we're getting somewhere.''

''I think we agreed we were alike in not forming lasting relationships, that's all.'' Was that what each of them had meant? Sera wasn't certain now.

Maisie shot her a knowing look.

"It just happened to come up in conversation," Sera said defensively.

"Okay. So when are you seeing him again?"

"I'm not sure. I thought maybe I'd get him to choose some paint samples tomorrow, if he has time. Or I do. It'll depend on whether or not they finish shooting in the morning."

It was Friday night, and it'd been a long day. The director and the writers had suddenly decided to change the setting of an upcoming scene from Dinah's living room to the apartment of one of her new friends, for which no set had been built.

There was a set now. It was nine forty-five in the evening, and Maisie and Sera had started at seven that morning. The carpenters and painters had finished an hour ago, and there were still the props to put in place before the set was ready for tomorrow morning's early shoot.

"Guess we'd better get back at it, or there won't be much point in going home tonight." Maisie yawned as they paid the bill and walked out into the balmy summer night.

People thronged the street. A busker sitting on the sidewalk strummed a guitar and sang a Spanish love song. Maisie tossed a handful of change into his hat, and he bowed to her.

"I really like this city. I wouldn't mind living here," she said as they made their way back to the studio. "In fact, I talked to a real estate agent the other day about buying an apartment. Apparently real estate is low right now.''

"You're really thinking of settling here in Vancouver?" Sera was astonished. Maisie had always said she was a free spirit; she didn't want to be tied down; as a set designer she needed to be able to relocate at a moment's notice. "What's made you change your mind all of a sudden?"

"Turning forty-eight, honey." There was an unaccustomed note of weariness in Maisie's raspy voice. "I'm getting tired of living like a vagabond. It's time I put down roots somewhere, and this town appeals to me. The natives are friendly, the energy's good, there's lots happening in theater and film, plenty of flights every day if I need to get to L.A. or other points south."

They edged past a group of tourists having a loud argument in German.

"Now, if I could just find an interesting, mature, sexually potent guy who liked fat women, I'd be set," Maisie added. She sounded as if she were only half joking.

"Do you think you'd ever get married again?"

"Marry again?" Maisie shook her head. "I don't think so. Three strikes are enough for me. I'm not good at marriage. I figure there's some secret to it that I never learned. Some couples manage to stay together for their entire lives. Look at your mom and dad, for instance. From what you say they still care for each other, and they've been married forever.''

''They're old-fashioned Italian,'' Sera said, as if that explained everything. ''Family's everything to them. I suppose my mother must have had times when she considered leaving—my father's not the easiest man to live with.'' Sera shook her head and rolled her eyes. ''Even I've had times when I wanted to murder him. He's overprotective, the typical Italian papa. He's got a terrible temper and he's so stubborn it makes you want to scream. He's pretty controlling. But he adores Mama, and I'm pretty sure it's mutual. We still catch them making out in the kitchen sometimes.''

''That's so sweet.''

Sera knew what was coming next, and she wished Maisie wouldn't ask.

''How about you, Sera? Think you'll ever get married?''

''I don't know.'' Sera had dreams just as every woman had, but they'd become shopworn in the past few years. ''I'd like to have kids someday,'' she confessed. ''But that's not a good reason to get married. And he'd have to be somebody I could absolutely trust.''

She thought of her sister. Thanks to Gemma, Sera had learned the hard way that trust was a rare commodity.

"You gonna tell Gemma about Ben, that you're decorating his apartment, et cetera, et cetera?"

"No. Absolutely not." Sera's reaction was powerful and instinctive. Even to consider telling Gemma made her uneasy. "She doesn't feel very attractive at the moment. I don't want to make her feel worse than she already does," she said, knowing that wasn't the real reason. "Besides, she may have a bit of a thing for Ben." She did suspect that.

Be honest, Sera, she chided herself. *You don't want Gemma to know because you don't trust her.* But she couldn't tell Maisie that, could she?

"Apparently women do fall for their doctors, although it's never happened to me. Are you two usually attracted to the same guys?"

"Sometimes. When we were younger. Men certainly were attracted to both of us. For some guys, twins are a challenge they just can't resist. They have fantasies about being in bed with both of us."

"Sick." Maisie was disgusted.

"I agree, but it's a fact of life." Old grievances stirred in Sera and threatened to surface. "It's as if we weren't separate people."

"Any idiot ever succeed in dating you both?"

"Once, in high school. And once was enough. I never got into a situation again where that was even possible."

"I can see where having somebody who resembles you so much could make it tough when you first meet a guy you go for,'' Maisie said thoughtfully. ''Every woman likes to feel her particular look is unique, whatever it is. When there're two of you, the guy would have to see beneath the surface right away, find your differences. Which of course is what all us females want anyhow, but the reality is that guys go on appearance a lot of the time. It usually takes them a while to get beyond that. Like forty years or thereabouts.''

They laughed, but Sera was glad that they'd reached the studio. Maisie's remarks had brought up disturbing memories of being ''one of the twins'' instead of an individual in her own right. In college, far away from Gemma, she'd never admitted to being a twin when she dated. She'd had several affairs, but whenever they threatened to become serious, Sera had ended them, using the excuse that her career demanded far too much of her emotional energy to allow for long-term commitment.

That was true, but it wasn't the whole story. The real truth was that she was a coward, and she knew it.

When anyone got too close, she ran. And if she kept on doing that, there was a better than even chance that she'd end up old and alone.

It wasn't a future she wanted to contemplate.

As she hung pictures on the walls of the set,

found a clock, arranged bric-a-brac so it seemed to have been in place for years, Sera thought about the conversation with Maisie and the surprising revelation that her friend was actually considering buying an apartment here in Vancouver.

Would the time come when she, too, decided that she needed to make a nest, Sera wondered. Biological clocks were becoming a cliché. Cliché or not, hers was ticking rapidly toward thirty.

Maisie knew for a fact she wasn't good at marriage, but Sera had never even tried it. To think about marriage you probably had to fall into love so totally fears were no longer a consideration.

Well, she hadn't come anywhere close to that. Maybe she needed to take a long, hard look at herself.

GEMMA HAD PLACED the hand mirror on the stand beside the bed, and for the third time in an hour, she picked it up and scrutinized her bruised and swollen face. At least the featureless mess she'd had before the operation was gone.

It was good to be out of the hospital, although staying here in her parents' house was a challenge. They were so sweet to her, but she was too accustomed to living on her own to really relax much.

Having the packing out of her nostrils and being able to breathe without the trach tube were heaven, though. Funny how a person's idea of pleasure could change. Before the accident partying and shopping for clothes had been tops on her fun list. Now pleasure meant watching the swelling on her face go down. Or, once her jaw healed, opening her mouth again.

God, this was so pathetic. She needed to get her life back.

"The mail arrived. Here's a letter for you." Maria came into the bedroom that Gemma and Sera had shared as children and handed her a white business-size envelope. The address was neatly typed. It was probably a bill, although how would anyone know she was here and not at her apartment?

"You want something to drink, *cara?*"

Maria had visited a health-food store and bought protein shakes and vitamins, which she mixed in a blender and insisted Gemma drink.

"You're skin and bone," Maria fussed. "It's not healthy to lose so much weight so fast. You've got to take in more calories. I'll go and fix you something."

Gemma carefully shook her head, but arguing with your mother when you couldn't talk was hard.

Maria hurried out, and a moment later Gemma heard the blender whining. Could a person actually *gain* weight with her jaw wired? Because if it was humanly possible, Maria, with her concoctions, would make sure it happened. Her mother made her crazy. Everyone made her crazy these days.

Irritably, Gemma tore open the envelope, unfolded the single sheet and scanned the typewritten words:

Beautiful Gemma
You burn like fire in my heart,
But don't know who I am.
Although I long to be your love,
I long to be your man.
I pause to think of you each day
I dream of you each night,
I close my eyes and there you are,
My joy, my hope, my light.

She read it through carefully, then read it once more. It was unsigned. She checked the envelope, but there was no return address, only the postmark. It had been mailed in Vancouver the previous day.

Beautiful Gemma. What kind of joke was that? And who would be so cruel? She read the simple words yet again, and for the first time since the accident, she felt the rush that came with knowing someone was attracted to her.

The poem wasn't a joke at all. Somebody was actually writing her love poetry. No one in her entire life had done that before.

She jumped up from the bed to show Maria, but at the door she changed her mind.

This was private. This was a secret she could

cherish, something to read over and over during the long nights when the demons haunted her. She didn't want anyone else looking at it.

Someone loved her, and she didn't even care that he hadn't signed his name to the declaration.

It was enough that he'd written his feelings down.

She'd have enough opportunity later to speculate on who it was. Right now, the sentiment was all she needed. It made her feel like her old self, and that was a gift beyond value.

CHAPTER EIGHT

THE FILMING was finished by noon on Saturday, and afterward Sera drove home and had a sandwich. She was about to call Ben about paint samples when her cell phone rang.

"Sera?"

She recognized his voice immediately.

"It's Ben. I know this is awfully short notice, but I wondered if you'd like to come to a barbecue this afternoon with my friends. Greg Brulotte and his wife, Lily, just called. They're having a few people over. I've mentioned you to them and they want to meet you."

Sera hesitated. The prospect of seeing Ben again was appealing, but being thrown into a group of strangers wasn't the way she'd prefer to do it.

"It'll be very casual, and I have to warn you my godson Stanley will be present."

"Grendel, too?"

"Absolutely."

"Okay, thank you, then I'll come."

"I knew that dog would earn his keep one of these days."

She laughed. "I was about to call you, actually. I wanted you to look at some paint samples."

"You pick out the paint, I'll say yes to whatever you choose."

"Here we go again." He'd been ridiculously grateful for the chairs she'd chosen for the office. Had sent her a bouquet of daisies and a funny thank-you card.

"What if you don't like the colors?"

"I will. I guarantee it. You're a genius at this stuff."

"Okay, but I still think you should check them out."

"Please, please don't make me."

She reluctantly agreed, and smiled when his voice took on an exuberant note as soon as they weren't talking about paint. "I'll come for you at five. Just give me the address."

She did.

She found her color samples, chose the shades for his loft in ten minutes, then spent the next hour frantically trying to figure out what to wear.

She wished she had time to race out and buy a new dress. She wished she was the sort of woman who had manicures and pedicures regularly.

She finally decided on a simple yellow cotton sundress with green daisies on it; it reminded her of the flowers Ben had sent. She painted her toenails and, using a cut lemon, got the worst of the paint stains off her hands.

He was ten minutes early and she was running late when the buzzer sounded.

She released the downstairs lock and quickly shoved her feet into bare sandals. She was giving her riotous curls a hasty finger comb when the doorbell rang.

"Hi." She knew she sounded breathless. "Come in. You can look at these colors while I get my handbag."

"Do I have to?" He was wearing a white polo shirt that emphasized his bronzed skin, and khaki shorts. His legs, she saw, were strong, well shaped and attractively hairy.

He gave the paint samples a cursory glance. "These are great." Then he tossed them on the small table by the door. "This is a nice place," he commented, gazing around at the plants and colorful cushions and cheap prints she'd used to make the rented apartment her own.

"Look around. I'll just be a minute." She raced into the bedroom and snatched up her straw bag.

"Bring a swimsuit. They have a pool," Ben called just when she thought she had everything. She swore under her breath and ransacked a drawer, hunting for her old navy tank suit. Why hadn't she bought a new one this summer?

With a breezy smile and an attempt at tranquillity

she was far from feeling, she hurried out to where he was waiting. He'd moved to the windows that overlooked Lost Lagoon and Stanley Park. "Great view."

"Nothing like yours, but it's okay. It's the reason I rented this. I like being able to see the trees and the water."

"Me, too." But he was gazing at her instead of the view. "You're beautiful, Sera."

She grimaced at him and crossed her eyes. "Your sight's failing."

He laughed. "Not with my glasses on it isn't." Catching her off guard, he bent toward her and kissed her briefly.

Her lips tingled and she felt a telltale blush come over her face. "Let's go." Being alone with him was far too tempting.

"Okay. I can't wait for you to meet my godson." He glanced at her dress. "That is washable, isn't it? I've learned never to go near Stanley in clothes that aren't washable. In fact, I've often thought Greg oughta issue hospital scrubs to whoever walks in his front door."

He took her hand and held it all the way down in the elevator. His truck was parked right out front in a No Parking zone.

"Hey, I didn't get a ticket." His surprise told Sera he usually did.

"I thought you'd be the hot-sports-car type," she

teased. Then added, "I'm green with envy. I always wanted a truck this color."

"I get ribbed about it all the time. I guess purple's funny for a truck."

"It's not purple. It's eggplant."

"Eggplant? *Eggplant.* Yuck. No wonder the guys have been giving me a bad time." His expression had her giggling. Grendel spied her just then and went into a frenzy of barking.

Sera waved at him through the tiny back window. "Can I say hello to him before we leave?"

Ben obligingly opened the door, undid the dog's safety harness and allowed him to leap out. Grendel licked Sera's hands and wound himself around her legs ecstatically.

"Okay, enough, you lovesick idiot. You're gonna get hair all over Sera's dress. You can drool at her through the back window."

Still nervous about meeting Ben's friends, Sera asked questions as soon as they drove off.

"Greg Brulotte's a doctor?"

"ER surgeon at St. Joe's. And Lily's an emergency-room nurse. They met on the job. She's pregnant with their second baby."

The ride wasn't long. The Brulotte family lived in Point Gray, one of the more exclusive areas in Vancouver. Sera remembered Ben's telling her that the impressive waterfront house with the circular drive had been his, and she admired it with that in mind.

No other cars were in the driveway.

"Are you sure we're not too early, Ben?"

He shook his head. "Greg and Lily asked us to come early. They want to get to know you before the others arrive."

As Ben rang the doorbell, she wondered again what she was getting into.

Grendel hung back.

"He's learned to be cautious around Stanley," Ben had time to say before a totally naked small boy opened the door and flung himself at Ben, wrapping first his arms and then his legs around him and trying to shinny up his body as if Ben were a climbing pole.

"Uncle Ben, I knew it was you. I saw you through the window." He had violet blue eyes and a thick head of unruly blond hair, but it was his animation that drew Sera's attention. His energy and exuberance shone around him like a bright light.

Ben grunted and steadied himself against the doorsill. Stanley was exceptionally tall and husky for three.

"Hey, tiger, what's going on? Where are your clothes?"

"Well, actually, I just had a poop upstairs," he

confided. He spoke with a slight lisp, and his huge eyes danced with mischief.

The expression of horror on Ben's face was genuine this time. "You did wipe afterward, didn't you, sport?"

Stanley gazed up at Ben, face angelic, smile devilish. "Nope, I came to ask you for help. See, I was sleeping and it woke me up, the poop."

"Oh, ssshh-oot. Where's your—" Ben's desperate question was cut short.

"Stanley Brulotte, you little imp." A tall woman with dramatically short silver blond hair and amazing green eyes hurried to the door. "Ben, come in, if you can even move with that lump hanging on you." She smiled at Sera. "I've given up apologizing for my son. Please do come in. You must be Sera. I'm Lily." She wiped a wet hand on her maternity sundress before extending it to Sera and warmly shaking her hand. Sera liked her immediately.

Lily Brulotte was both beautiful and hugely pregnant. She took her son's hands and, with some difficulty, peeled him off Ben. "Say hello to Ms. Cardano, you exhibitionist, and then go upstairs and tell Daddy to find you some clothes."

"Hi, Stanley. You can call me Sera." She smiled at the little boy. She loved kids, and this one was obviously unusual. He gave her a shy grin and a long, considering look, then turned to his mother. "I'll go scare Daddy. Okay, Mommy?"

"Be my guest."

Stanley charged off, and Lily gestured down a sunny hallway. "I'm just finishing the salads. Let's go in the kitchen. You can cut up potatoes for me, Ben. Greg will be down as soon as he wrestles that kid into some clothes."

They walked down a hall that was a minefield of abandoned toys. The family-style kitchen lay at the back of the house, its patio doors opening wide to a cedar deck equipped with a child's wading pool and even more brightly colored toys. Below the deck, Sera glimpsed a large swimming pool, and beyond that stretched the inlet, sparkling in the afternoon sunshine.

"Sera, sit down here so we can get acquainted." Lily was tearing lettuce into a huge wooden bowl.

"Why don't I peel these potatoes, and Ben can chop them." Sera was at home in a busy kitchen; she'd grown up helping with the huge Sunday meals her mother and aunts took turns preparing.

"If you don't mind, I'd appreciate it." Lily gave her a thankful smile and handed Sera a knife. "Ben tells me you're a set designer for a sitcom taped here in Vancouver. He also said you chose those scrumptious new chairs in his office. All his friends and patients are grateful to you for that."

Sera shot Ben a glance, curious what else he

might have said about her. All she could see was
the top of his head, bent diligently over the potatoes.

The sound of small feet pounding down the stairs
and along the hall announced the reappearance of
Stanley. He raced into the kitchen, then stopped
abruptly and struggled hard until he'd succeeded in
pulling down the madras shorts he wore.

"Look, Uncle Ben, I got big-boy underwear
now, just like you wear." He turned a full circle,
stumbling over the shorts around his ankles. His
chubby face was wreathed in smiles, and his small
bottom was encased in bright-red Calvins.

It was all Sera could do not to laugh, but she
took her cue from Ben. Without a trace of a smile,
he studied the small boy and nodded solemnly.
"You really are a big fella, tiger. Now you and I
have matching underwear."

Sera caught his eye and couldn't resist winking
suggestively.

A tall, handsome man with curly dark hair and
deep-set brown eyes followed Stanley into the
kitchen.

"Hi, Sera, welcome." He was warm and charming. "I'm Greg, the father of this miniature male
stripper." He took Sera's hand in his for a moment
and gave her a wide smile, then helped his son pull
his shorts back up. Then he went over to his wife,
casually pressed a kiss on the back of her neck and

ruffled her hair. "How's it goin', sweetheart? What can I do?"

The way he touched her, the tender note in his voice, telegraphed his devotion to her.

"You can rinse the strawberries and then use your surgical skills at cutting them up for the short-cake." Lily smiled at him, and here, too, love was palpable.

Their visible affection for each other set the tone in this household, Sera concluded as the afternoon wore on. There was much laughter and bantering as everyone helped prepare for the party, and by the time other guests began to arrive, Sera felt accepted and totally at ease.

Two other couples came, both as friendly and outgoing as Greg and Lily. As Sera got to know them, she realized they were connected in various ways with St. Joseph's hospital.

Lily's brother, Kaleb Sullivan, was a fireman, married to Frannie, a social worker at the hospital. They had a two-year-old named Harry and an older girl, Zoe, whom Sera learned was Kaleb's from a previous marriage. Zoe was extraordinarily lovely, with feather-soft hair and huge eyes.

Thea and Wade Keenan were the parents of Marshall, a husky, serious five-year-old, and adorable five-month-old twins, Della and Frank. Sera admired them and silently thought how lucky they were not to be identical. She didn't say anything about being a twin herself, and she noted that Ben didn't mention it, either.

Wade, who'd been severely injured in a motorcycle accident, was a counselor with a private practice, but he also worked with patients at St. Joe's who'd sustained spinal-cord injuries. He walked with a cane and had a pronounced limp, and he told Sera that Ben had done an incredible job of repairing his hands and his face.

"My sister was in an accident recently. Her face was badly injured," Sera heard herself saying. "Ben operated on her. She looks so much better already."

"Don't reinforce the fact that he's a genius. It takes us weeks to get him back to normal afterward," Greg joked.

It was almost impossible for Sera to believe that Wade's wife, Thea, had produced three children and was still breast-feeding twins; she was incredibly slim and strikingly lovely. Not surprisingly, she'd been a fashion model. She cheerfully announced that she was taking time off from her career to raise her kids. "And once they're ready for school, I'll be too old to do much modeling, even if I get Ben to remove all the loose skin on my face and belly," she laughed. "So I'm going to set up my own agency. I'm doing courses in business admin at night school."

Sera found these people intriguing. All the

women were dynamic, each pursuing careers while juggling the demands of young children.

Sera couldn't help but contrast their get-togethers with Cardano gatherings, where the women and children segregated in one area and the men in another, and the brunt of the child care and all the cooking falling to the women.

These men, on the other hand, shared equally in the household chores, from supervising the toddlers to helping with dinner. They obviously enjoyed doing so. To witness equality in action was refreshing for her.

The quantity of kids made for a noisy, hectic gathering. Ben was attentive to her, but he didn't hover, and she appreciated that. Everyone seemed genuinely interested in her job, and Sera found the conversation fast paced and stimulating.

She cradled one of the twins, loving the smell of the small baby and the warmth of the tiny body. The baby had just fallen asleep when Ben appeared at her side.

"Can I lure you away for a swim before we eat?" he asked. "You and I are the only ones free to enjoy the pool, so we might as well take advantage of it."

Sera nodded, and Wade quickly held his arms out to take his baby. "I can't believe there're actually people who can go for a swim without arranging baby-sitters and feeding schedules or having life-

guards stand by,'' he said, pretending to complain.
His proud smile as he shouldered his daughter
showed that he didn't for a moment consider his
life a hardship.

CHAPTER NINE

THE POOL WAS SET into a rock wall on one side and securely protected by a sturdy wire fence on the remaining three sides. The Brulottes had planted climbing rosebushes to disguise the fencing, and glorious pink and yellow flowers perfumed the hot afternoon air. The sound of the other guests' voices and occasional bursts of laughter or cries from a child floated down, but Sera felt a delicious sense of intimacy in being there alone with Ben.

One assessing glance confirmed that he looked even better half naked than he did clothed. His broad chest was matted with hair, his body trim and well muscled. He waved when she appeared after getting into her swimsuit in the change room adjacent to the pool. She walked past him and slid quickly into the water, self-conscious about her untanned skin.

They swam for a while and then rested, cool water lapping at their shoulders.

"Isn't this great? I'll bet you missed the pool when you moved out of this house," Sera said.

"Yup. But now I get to use it whenever I like

without the headache of upkeep. Although Stanley usually comes in with me, and trying to keep him from drowning sort of balances out not having to clean the pool, so Greg got the best of the deal after all. That kid has no fear. His favorite trick is to walk straight to the deep end, holler 'Watch me, Uncle Ben' and jump in before I can get down there. He knows how to hold his breath, but it still scares me half to death. A couple of occasions I've had to leap straight in with my glasses on.''

This was the first time Sera had seen Ben without his glasses. He looked different—just as handsome but less professional. A little vulnerable, which Sera found sexy.

''Have you always worn glasses?'' She clung to the edge of the pool, stretching her legs, enjoying the heat of the sun on her back. He pulled himself smoothly out of the water and sat on the edge, reaching a hand to haul her up beside him.

''Since I was in college. They're a damned nuisance.''

''They really are,'' she agreed heartily. ''Gemma and I were both myopic. We must have been born that way. I had laser surgery four years ago to correct my eyesight and Gemma had her eyes done shortly afterward. Being able to see without glasses or contacts is a miracle. Ever think of having the surgery?''

"Never." His response and the certainty in his tone surprised her.

"Why's that?" She slipped on the sunglasses she'd remembered to bring. "You're a surgeon—you're aware it's a really simple operation."

"Umm." He nodded. "I just wouldn't ever undergo any sort of elective surgery," he admitted with an abashed grin. "Having one of my colleagues operate on me at my request is my worst nightmare."

She thought at first he was joking, but when she turned and looked at him, she realized he was absolutely serious.

A surgeon with a dread of surgery?

Ben Halsey was a fascinating, complicated man.

Sitting beside him in the sunshine, their bare, sun-warmed shoulders touching, thighs brushing, feet side by side gently sloshing the water, Sera realized she wanted to know much more about him. She wanted to know *everything* about him.

She was also certain she wanted to make love with him. Not today, but at some point in the not-too-distant future. He took her hand in his, and the physical connection intensified the electricity between them.

Ben was aware of it. She could tell by the way his breathing became uneven when their skin made contact. She could tell by the intense expression in his eyes each time he looked at her. Strange, she thought dreamily, how bodies knew long before minds admitted the truth.

She did her best to overlook the silent, sensual messages and concentrate instead on what they were talking about.

"How can you have a thing about surgery, Ben? You're a surgeon yourself."

"I'm totally irrational. I admit it. See, doctors make the worst patients. Any nurse will tell you that. You oughta ask Lily what Greg was like after his accident."

Ben blew out a breath and shook his head. "He was so ornery he even made *me* want to punch him out, and he's my best buddy. The nurses agreed he was the worst patient they'd ever seen. They gave him a certificate attesting to that. Quite a few reached the point where they wouldn't even deal with him. There were only two nurses who weren't intimidated by him."

"Lily, and who else?"

Ben shook his head. "Nope, Lily wasn't doing his nursing care. The Krupps twins were the ones who whipped him into shape." In hilarious detail he described for her two militant nurses who'd managed to intimidate Greg.

Sera laughed at his story and thought of the man she'd met that day—the loving husband, the doting father, the entertaining, generous, charming host.

He was easygoing, reasonable. "You're exaggerating."

Ben shook his wet head and pressed a hand to his bare, hairy chest. "God's truth, I swear. He was way beyond obnoxious. Most doctors are if we land in hospital. I guess it's because we know how many things can go wrong. And we're inclined to be egotists. We figure nobody could possibly do anything as well as we'd do it ourselves. Which is at the bottom of my phobia about letting anybody cut into me."

"But that doesn't make sense."

"I know. So I'm not always a sensible man, so what?" He grinned and in one lithe motion levered off the edge and into the water, sending it cascading over her. "C'mon back in. I'll race you to the end."

It was no contest. Sera was more than a competent swimmer, but Ben had raw power and a killer instinct for competition. She liked the fact that he didn't hold back or pretend to let her win; he threw himself into the game as if his reputation depended on it.

They found a ball and tossed it back and forth, tested their ability to swim underwater from one end of the pool to the other and then back and finally stretched out side by side on chaises longues, catching their breath and drying off in the sunshine.

"So, Ben Halsey, besides being irrational, clearly

you don't like to lose,'' Sera commented. ''Did you grow up with a pile of brothers?''

''Only one. David's three years older than I am. He's a lawyer in Toronto. We were pretty competitive, all right. I guess we still are in some ways. He's married to a lawyer. They're partners in the same firm.'' He grimaced. ''Now, there's competition for you—marrying somebody who does the exact same job you do.''

''I can't imagine living with another set designer. That would be a recipe for disaster. And look at actors. Their track records are pretty dismal.'' She remembered that Ben had been married at some point. ''What did your wife do?''

''Vera was a nurse.'' His voice changed when he talked about his marriage. The bantering was gone. ''She worked on maternity at St. Joe's.''

''So you were both in medicine. I guess that would cause problems.''

''*I* caused problems.'' There was wry humor in his tone, but Sera could tell that beneath it he was totally sincere. ''We married during my final year of internship, after knowing each other all of six weeks. It only took six more for me to realize I'd made a terrible mistake. I wasn't ready for marriage, and I don't think she was, either.''

''How long did it last?''

''Ten months. I had a chance to go to India and work extensively on burn patients. She didn't want to go. Our relationship was falling apart, so I started divorce proceedings before I left.''

"At least you were both mature enough to realize the marriage was a mistake. And you didn't have kids to complicate matters." Sera wondered what Vera was like, where she was now.

"Vera miscarried in her fourth month."

"Oh, Ben, I'm sorry. That must have been heart-breaking for you." She'd seen today how he adored Stanley.

"I was relieved." She hadn't heard such harsh-ness before in his voice. "See, I hadn't planned on a baby. Vera got pregnant deliberately when the India thing came up, and I felt trapped and mad, because I knew it was her way of keeping me here, tied to her." He turned toward her and lifted his sunglasses so she could see his green eyes. They held no laughter, only an old bitterness. "It was a big relief to me when she lost our baby. I told her I wanted a divorce and then I took off for India, feeling as if I'd solved a tough problem."

Sera wondered why he was telling her all this. It obviously wasn't something he brought up in casual conversation.

"Within a month, Vera attempted suicide. I'd suspected she was mentally unstable right after we married, but I hadn't realized how seriously."

Sera could only shake her head in horror.

"She survived, just barely." He was silent for a while, and Sera didn't know what to say.

At last he sighed and added, "It was a long while ago. I've never seen her since. I was in India when she was in the psych ward, and when I got back she'd moved in with her parents. I tried to call her a couple of times, but they made it pretty plain I wasn't to have any contact with her. Time passed, and I never really tried anymore."

"Where is she now?"

"North Vancouver. According to the hospital grapevine, she never fully recovered. She's never worked again as a nurse or remarried. Her parents are dead now. Apparently she lives with her sister and works in a bakery. I feel bad about that, because she was well liked at St. Joe's, really good at her job. Her family still blames me."

"How long ago was all this?"

"Twelve years."

"Seems to me that's time enough for everyone to get over it. Maybe she needs counseling." But even as she said it, Sera knew there were things you just didn't get over. Look at her and Gemma; she'd never gotten over their differences. Who was she to judge Vera? And it was all too clear that Ben still felt guilty.

"It wasn't your fault," she offered. That was all she could think of to say.

"Not entirely, maybe. But I certainly wasn't innocent, either.'' He drew in a long breath. ''I did a lot of soul-searching and decided I was a selfish bastard who shouldn't involve himself in serious relationships ever again.'' He added in a deliberate tone, ''I've stuck to that, Sera. I don't see marriage or babies in my future.''

It took a minute, but then it dawned on her he was giving her a blatantly clear message. She was suddenly insulted and furious with him. How dare he assume she needed warning? How dare he assume he was irresistible to her? Even though he was.

''Are you telling me not to fall for you, Ben?'' She said it quietly, but there was ice in her tone. ''Because if you are, don't flatter yourself.''

He looked disconcerted. ''I guess I just want you to know all about me, good, bad, awful.'' He was watching her with that intensity she found both arousing and disturbing, and now she resented the way he made her feel.

''But you're warning me, as well,'' she insisted.

He frowned. ''I'm trying to be honest with you is all. I'm telling you right up-front what kind of guy I am, so there's no misunderstandings between us.''

Your Dr. Halsey is a love-'em-and-leave-'em sort of guy. Sera could hear Maisie's voice in her head. Why was she so outraged that he'd spelled it out for her? She wasn't about to propose to him, for cripes sake.

All the same, she was angry. "What makes you think—"

Before Sera could continue, Greg leaned over the deck railing and hollered, "I've been slaving away over a fiery barbecue and the food's ready. Stanley'll escort you both to dinner."

A second later, the little boy made his way carefully down the stairs toward them.

"Daddy says we gotta eat *now,* Uncle Ben." He took Ben's hand with one of his and waited until Sera got to her feet to put his small, damp fingers shyly in hers.

"Where's Grendel gotten to, Stanley?" Sera did her best to subdue her exasperation with Ben.

"He's hiding under the steps. He won't play with me. He don't like playing dinosaur. Why I couldn't go swimming with you, Uncle Ben? Can I go next time?"

"Next time for sure, partner."

They walked up the stairs with the boy chattering between them, and when they reached the top Greg handed them each a laden plate.

Although the food was delicious and everyone else laughed a lot, the shine had gone out of the afternoon for Sera. She was relieved when Ben suggested they leave soon after they'd eaten. On the drive back to her apartment neither of them said much. When he stopped the truck, he asked if she wanted him to take another look at the color samples.

She refused, understanding that it was his way of asking whether he could come up. "I sort of promised Mom and Dad I'd keep Gemma company tonight," she improvised, reaching for the door handle.

"Sera." He grabbed her wrist. "If I sounded like an arrogant SOB back there, I'm sorry." His voice softened. "The fact is, I'm very attracted to you, and I want absolute honesty between us, so we know exactly where we stand."

"And where do you think that is, Ben?" She glared at him, aware at the same time that Grendel had his nose pressed tight against the window, eyeing her with utter devotion.

Why couldn't this man be more like his goofy dog?

"I'd like to go to bed with you, Ben. I find you sexually attractive," she admitted in the most level and reasonable tone she could muster. "I also find it insulting that you'd assume I'd want more than that. I thought we discussed the fact that we're both career oriented, that our jobs come ahead of relationships in our lives." But if that was true, what had upset her so much?

"You're right. We did discuss that, and I was way out of line bringing it up again." He hadn't released his hold on her wrist. "So, are you going to forgive me or not?"

There was both challenge and promise in his green eyes, and for a long moment, Sera debated. The rational part of her brain knew that she ought to climb out of the truck now and run fast and far away from this dangerous man.

But even the fingers lightly holding her wrist made her heart beat faster, and she acknowledged that there wasn't any decision to make. Her heart had made it already.

"I forgive you," she said, unable to resist adding in a snippy tone, "just don't let it happen again."

"Anybody ever mention you have a temper?" He smiled at her an instant, and then with a suddenness that made her gasp, he dragged her into his arms and kissed her.

CHAPTER TEN

BEN HELD HER CLOSE, cursing himself for the inept way he'd mismanaged things. What the hell had possessed him, blurting out all that ancient history about his marriage and then segueing straight into his damned declaration of independence? He couldn't remember ever being as clumsy about it as he'd been today. Sera was absolutely justified in being royally ticked off with him.

He hadn't planned to discuss it with her yet, and certainly not the way it had happened. He'd wanted to know her better, and the barbecue had seemed a perfect opportunity. The problem was, Sera had a way of getting under his skin, drawing out confidences he ordinarily wouldn't make. He still wasn't exactly sure how the disastrous conversation had come about.

Now, with her in his arms, he wanted nothing more than to take her up to her apartment and spend the rest of the evening making passionate love, but he'd blown that possibility.

You idiot, Halsey.

She ended the embrace, moving away, reaching

for the door handle. He put a restraining hand on her arm.

"Wait just a moment. I'll walk you out. When can I see you again?" He tried to remember what his week was like. He had several meetings he absolutely couldn't skip. "How about dinner, maybe a show? I'll check my schedule. We can decide which night."

She hesitated, and he realized how very much he wanted to go on seeing her. "What about tomorrow night?" He'd just get out of whatever engagements he had.

His heart sank when she shook her head.

"This week's crazy. We're having to shoot several episodes because some of the actors have other commitments. I'll probably be working most evenings."

"Lunch, then." He'd have Dana postpone a few appointments. "Tuesday?"

Still she hesitated, and he was afraid she was about to refuse. "I'd love that tour of the set you promised me." That was devious of him, but he wasn't about to let her walk out of his life.

"Okay, Tuesday."

Relief flooded through him. Now all he had to do was keep from putting his sandal in his mouth anew.

He walked Sera to the door of her building and kissed her again, lightly.

"See you Tuesday."

He watched her go inside. She turned and waved at him before she boarded the elevator, and he felt like throwing his arms above his head in a triumphant salute.

He'd salvaged the day after all. He was back in the truck before it occurred to him to wonder why it was so necessary that he see her again. There were other women in Vancouver.

But none of them were Sera.

GEMMA'S APPOINTMENT was at 9:15 on Tuesday morning, and she was pleased that Ben seemed to be waiting for her, ushered her into his office himself, instead of having the office nurse do it.

"Gemma, it's a real pleasure to see you." He touched her arm and smiled, meeting her eyes. "How have you been?"

There was more to the question than simply a doctor's concern; she was sure of it. Ben really wanted to know how *she* was, Gemma Cardano, not just the patient with the wired jaw and the reconstruction. The way he looked at her, the tone of his voice, the expression on his face—all made her feel attractive, womanly, in spite of what the mirror reflected. So she took the pad and pen he offered and instead of just scribbling "Okay," she told him how scared she was that the bruising on her temples and cheekbones wouldn't go away, that the headaches were fewer and further between but the pain in her jaw made tears pour down her cheeks sometimes, that she hated going out because of how people stared.

He listened and then addressed every single concern, calming her fears, erasing her worries one by one.

"Come and sit on this stool. We'll make sure everything is healing as it should." He stood so close she could feel the warmth of his body, even faintly smell his aftershave or deodorant, she wasn't sure which. It reminded her of oranges, and when he asked if her sense of smell was coming back at all, she nodded and scribbled that down, and he tossed back his head and laughed.

"Nice to know it's working. Not just your sniffer—my deodorant."

He put a hand on her shoulder as he leaned over her to examine her face. His strong fingers were gentle, sensitive, as he tipped her head back with one finger under her chin and searched her face.

Her heart was hammering, and for the first time since the accident, she felt the stirrings of sexual response, and a wave of heat ran through her.

"This looks amazingly good. You're healing really fast." He stroked a finger down the side of her face, tenderly tracing the red line that was all that remained of the gash that had been there. "I doubt we'll have to do any further work on this. The scar will be nearly invisible. You have great skin, great recuperative ability.''

There was something special, something warm and loving and intimate, in the way he spoke to her, and the memory of his voice lingered long after she left the office.

The timbre of it, the intonation he used when he said her name, echoed again on Wednesday evening as Gemma waited until her parents left for the movie before going into her bedroom and taking out the familiar envelope that had arrived that afternoon. She hadn't had a chance to really concentrate on the words because Maria had been nearby when the mailman brought it.

Now she impatiently unfolded the single sheet of paper, heart pounding in anticipation:

Gemma—
I lie in an empty bed,
While shadows flow around me,
Your perfume fresh in my nostrils.
The memory of your voice,
Whispering in my inner ear,
Words not spoken.
How will I get from dark to daylight
Without you, Gemma?

She sighed and reread it. The guy had such a way with words. She'd never been much on poetry, couldn't understand most of it, but these poems were different.

They were about her, written *for* her, and they touched something deep inside. This was the fourth one; she was getting one almost every day now. The arrival of the mailman had become the focus of her entire life.

She'd hidden the poems in her bureau, in the carved wooden box she'd used to hide her cigarettes when she was twelve, and she still hadn't told a living soul.

This whole thing was too new, too special, to share with anyone. She'd let Sera in on it when the right time came, but for now she just wanted to keep it private and think about whoever was sending these beautiful love messages to her.

She thought she knew. She was *sure* she knew. It hadn't taken much effort to figure it out, either. There was only one man in her life now who was sophisticated, smart and verbal enough to write such things: Ben Halsey.

Her own Dr. Ben. She could see him clearly in her mind's eye—his caring smile, the attentive and gentle expression in his green eyes. She could hear his voice repeating each word. She understood that as long as she was his patient, of course he couldn't say anything directly to her, which was why he sent her the poetry, instead.

He was waiting until she was completely healed,

until she was no longer his patient, to reveal that he cared about her romantically.

She longed for that moment to arrive. She'd been guzzling down every drop of the horrible stuff Maria blended for her, in the hope that it really would speed up the healing. Now she had a powerful reason to get better fast.

"Gemma, hi, it's me." Sera's tap on the bedroom door startled her. She stuffed the poem into the box with the others and shoved it back in the drawer a bare instant before her sister came in.

"How ya doin'?" Sera gave her a hug and a smile. "We finished a while ago. I thought I'd come over and talk you into going for a walk, it's so nice outside. How about it?"

Gemma shook her head, and Sera looked exasperated.

"You've gotta start getting some exercise or soon you won't have any muscle tone left. Your skin'll sag and your thighs will have those ugly ripples."

So far, Gemma had refused to step foot out the door of her parents' house except for trips to Ben's office. She hated the way strangers gawked at her, hated their fascinated horrified glance that telegraphed *What the hell happened to you?* They'd look away quick, but clearly it was a big effort not to stare. The worst part was knowing that before this had happened to her, she'd done exactly the

same thing when she'd encountered someone out of
the ordinary. She vowed she'd never do it again.
From now on, she'd look, and smile, and say something that made the person at least feel human.

"What d'ya think, Em? About that walk?"

Gemma knew Sera was expecting her to refuse
again. It felt good to change her mind and indicate
yes and see the surprise on her sister's face. It felt
good to find her shoes and follow Sera out into the
soft summer evening.

"This week's been busy. We've been filming extra episodes because Lorelei and Bertram have parts
in a movie, and they've got to go back to L.A. next
week. We're almost done this series anyway.
There'll likely be only a couple more weeks' work.
But there're two low-budget movies that'll be shot
in and around Vancouver. It's pretty likely our
crew'll get hired on one or both, Maisie says. It
would be nice to have a week or two off between,
although that probably won't happen."

Gemma knew that Lorelei was the actress who
played the lead role in *Dinah*. Gemma had met her
once. She was sort of dumpy, not at all the way she
looked on TV.

Gemma envied Sera's getting to meet movie
stars, her knowing what went on behind the cameras, but who'd want to live in L.A.? Vancouver
was home, and Gemma planned to stay here forever.

A woman passed them, giving Gemma "the look." Gemma ignored her. What did it matter now that people stared? She had someone who cared about her, someone special who wasn't interested in her just because she was sexy and knew how to have a good time.

"Mama told me Jack comes by to see you a lot. He seems like a real nice guy. She said you guys play poker. You ever tell him Uncle Bernardo taught us all the tricks? Or do you let him win once in a while just to keep him interested?"

A niggle of guilt threatened Gemma's newfound excitement and happiness, but she shoved it to the back of her mind. After all, she wasn't promising Jack anything by allowing him to come to the house nearly every night, was she? All she was doing was enabling him to work off his guilt; if he chose to spend his evenings playing cards with her and losing, that was up to him, wasn't it?

Jack didn't have much of a social life anyway, as far as she could figure; he'd made it abundantly clear the times she'd gone out with him that he wasn't interested in partying.

Too bad, because he was kind of sexy, in his own inarticulate way. He was different from the men she usually dated; that was for sure. He was forty-one for starters, a full thirteen years older than she. He drove a vintage Land Rover he'd fixed up himself and he put most of what he earned into materials for a big old house he'd bought and was remodeling.

He was a different sort of guy. Not her sort at all.

Ben, too, was different, although he probably had a fast car, and for sure he had money; everybody knew plastic surgeons made tons of money. But he had a depth that all the men she'd dated in the past had lacked.

Except Jack, and he didn't really count.

She'd fallen in love a couple of times before, but never as with Ben; none of the men had ever been this romantic. She'd thought for a while Raymond was romantic, but she'd been so mistaken.

Raymond was the loser she'd married. He'd bought her flowers and perfume, and she'd believed he was strong and capable, someone who could handle her, someone who saw past her fast mouth and wild ways to the insecure kid she hid so well from the world. Instead, he'd been a world-class liar and a con artist, and in the end a coward, as well. He'd smacked her around once.

Only once. Gemma had called her dad, who'd put the fear of death into Raymond and then spent a fortune on a lawyer who got an order to keep him from coming near her ever again. She'd never told Sera about that, and she'd begged her dad not to tell either Mama or Sera.

He'd given her a lecture, but when it was over

Papa had promised, and Aldo always kept his promises.

"I was thinking about you and Raymond the other day, how you met him and got married within a month."

Gemma's whole body tensed. Sometimes having a twin was both uncanny and dangerous. It felt at times like this that Sera was actually reading her mind, and in a way she was. They picked up stuff from each other; they always had.

"I remember envying you so much when you got married," Sera was saying. "I know it didn't work out, but still, you tried it. Marriage, I mean. I'd never have the guts to just go ahead and get married."

Not guts, Gemma wanted to say. Not brains, either.

Blind stupidity was more like it.

Sera was way too smart to get herself into a mess like Raymond. And imagine St. Sera *envying* Gemma anything.

The truth was, it was always she who'd envied Sera. Her sister had a stability that she herself lacked, an ability to zero in on what she wanted and go after it, follow it through and make it work for her. There was a core of integrity in Sera that Gemma had always known was missing in her personality, no matter how much alike they were in other ways. It was as if nature had slipped up; instead of giving them exactly the same personalities, Sera had received the best of the deal.

Good twin, bad twin. It didn't take a genius to figure out which was which in the Cardano family.

"Think you'll ever try marriage again?" Sera turned to look at her sister, waiting for a response.

Gemma hesitated and then she nodded. She would; of course she would. She'd marry Ben in a minute if the time came. It would be such a relief to belong to someone like him, to just relax and be taken care of, not to have to chase affection or try to prove she was worthy.

"Maisie's talking about buying an apartment or a condo in Vancouver," Sera said next. "I guess it started me thinking about settling down someday."

Gemma felt the familiar surge of jealousy and betrayal she always experienced when Sera talked about Maisie. Weren't the two of them, Sera and Gemma, supposed to be each other's best friends? Nature had intended it that way; why else had they been born identical twins? But Sera had gone away since they'd grown up, not just physically, but emotionally, as well. And she'd given the intimacy that rightfully belonged to Gemma to a stranger. The one positive thing about getting smashed in the face was that it had brought her and Sera close again.

"I don't know if I could do a good job of being married," Sera was saying thoughtfully. "I've always figured marriage meant having to give up a big part of yourself. I felt sorry for Mama when we were growing up. She seemed to always put everybody else's needs first, especially Papa's. And he expects it.''

Gemma didn't think that way at all. She'd spent more time with her mother and father lately than she had since early childhood. She'd done more listening and watching than ever before, and she'd noticed things about her parents.

Getting smashed had done that to her, made her notice stuff she'd been too busy to look at before.

Maria and Aldo cared about each other on all sorts of different levels, and somehow they'd managed to use their differences to make their union interesting and strong. She didn't think Mama did anything she didn't want to do. Sure, Papa was old-fashioned and had definite ideas about how everybody should act, but Mama had a way of making him see reason.

But then, Sera had always been closer to their mother than Gemma. Maybe Mama had told Sera things she hadn't told Gemma.

Maria had always been able to see Gemma's bad side, and that had caused lots of tension between them. Aldo had been Gemma's confidant. She'd always known that whatever mess she got into, her papa would be there for her. He might rant and rave, but in the end he always helped.

''I went to a barbecue last weekend, mostly married couples with little kids. The guys did as much diapering and cooking as the women did. That's the sort of relationship I want,'' Sera was saying. ''If I ever find the right guy.''

At that moment, Gemma desperately wanted to tell Sera that she thought *she* had met the right guy, but she didn't have a damned pen or paper with her. She touched Sera's shoulder and turned around, even though they'd gone only a few blocks.

Besides wanting to confide in her sister about Ben, Gemma knew Jack was coming over in a little while. He'd offered to teach her how to use the Internet and he was bringing over his laptop computer. She'd never been interested in computers before, but having Ben explain how he'd used computer imaging to fix her face intrigued her. She wanted to learn all she could about Ben's work so she'd have something to talk to him about—when she could talk again.

''I happened to see Dr. Halsey yesterday afternoon,'' Sera said offhandedly. ''He told me you'd been in his office in the morning. He said he's really pleased with how you're healing. You do look great, Em. Not much longer now, and your jaw will be healed, too, and we can really talk again. This one-sided conversation is a royal pain.''

Gemma was instantly on guard. Instead of confiding in Sera, when they got home she found a pen and paper and scribbled *How did you happen to see Dr. Ben yesterday?*

"Oh, he dropped by the set. He wanted to see how a television sitcom was made."

Alarms went off in Gemma's head and heart. Sera liked him. Gemma knew immediately, despite her sister's attempt at sounding ultracasual. In big, scrawling letters she printed *Hands off on Ben, Sera. I really go for him, and I'm pretty sure he feels the same.*

Sera took a long time to reply. Her head was bent over the paper, so Gemma couldn't see her expression.

At last she looked up, straight into Gemma's eyes. She looked for a long time and then she nodded.

Gemma knew her smile wasn't genuine, though.

"Okay, Gemma. We're not gonna disagree over a man." There was a tiny catch in her voice, and Gemma cursed the wires in her jaw. It was so hard for her to communicate through writing.

While she was trying to figure out how much else to tell Sera, the doorbell rang and Jack arrived.

Sera talked to him for a brief moment about the computer he'd brought and then, with a goodbye that Gemma knew Sera intended to be light and cheerful, she left.

Jack was an excellent teacher, and Gemma quickly became engrossed in the workings of the computer. Within a few moments, excited by learning a new skill, she'd forgotten the awkward episode with her sister.

SERA DROVE BLINDLY to a small park not far from her parents' house. She turned off the motor and let her shoulders slump, as she struggled with the conflicting feelings that coursed through her.

In spite of the sickness in her gut, the overwhelming sense of unfairness, she had to make sense of what had just occurred.

She forced herself to deal with just the facts, to put aside her raw and painful emotions.

Gemma was attracted to Ben, perhaps as powerfully as Sera herself was.

Her sister had been severely injured, in a fashion that every woman shuddered even to imagine. Gemma's self-esteem was at an all-time low.

Was Ben attracted to Gemma? Sera thought not, but how could she be certain? Something more than just her sister's imagination must be involved here. Injured or not, Gemma was no fool, certainly not where men were concerned. She wouldn't have a thing for Ben unless he'd given her *some* encouragement, would she?

That Ben could have shown her sister some of the same affection he was showing her hurt most of all.

And this wasn't really about Ben, Sera reminded

herself sternly. It was about her and her sister. It was about the genetic cell-deep similarity that doomed them to fall in love with the same men.

She stared blindly out for a long time, at kids on the play equipment, at soccer players madly chasing a ball, at young moms pushing their strollers.

Gradually, the light faded and the park emptied. The street lamps came on, and the warmth of the summer day began to fade as night settled on the city.

It was after ten when at last she started the car, backed up and pulled into traffic, knowing exactly what she would do, what she had to do.

As she'd told her sister earlier, she wouldn't compete with her over a man.

CHAPTER ELEVEN

MAISIE'S APARTMENT had character but no elevator. After ten minutes, Sera was still breathing heavily from the three sets of stairs she'd climbed to reach it.

"It's not the bloody set I'm concerned about, luv. It's you," Maisie declared. "There's not much left to do. I can handle it fine. If you want to leave a couple days early, it's not a big deal. The filming's nearly done anyway. But what's the hurry?"

Maisie scowled at Sera and wrapped the voluminous terry robe tighter around her middle. She'd been in the bathtub when Sera rang to say she needed to see her right away. There was a trail of wet footprints on the rug leading from the bathroom to the door.

Ordinarily, Sera would never have barged in with a scant ten minutes' notice this late at night. But she had to settle this before she lost her nerve.

"You're running away from this Halsey guy, aren't you?" Maisie narrowed her eyes at Sera. "What's that bastard done to you?"

"Nothing. I just need to go back to Los Angeles."

"He get too close? You start to care more than you want to?" Maisie wasn't going to drop the matter, and Sera was too heartsick to put up much of a defense.

"Something like that."

Maisie shook her head. "Damned men, they really screw up a gal's life. And her career. You're walking away from the chance to do the sets for those movies, remember. Now, there's a cool career move if ever I saw one."

Sera knew. It hurt her to think about it. "I'm sure I can find something in L.A."

"Maybe yes, maybe no. Come in and sit down. We'll have a cup of tea and figure this out." Maisie led the way into the kitchen and put the kettle on. "I know this producer in San Diego—Pasquale Young. We had a thing together once in another lifetime. We keep in touch. He called me a couple weeks ago. He's planning a pilot for a television drama set in the twenties and he thought maybe I'd like to do the sets. I would, too, if it didn't mean working with him. We fight all the time when we're not screwing our brains out. I can't take it anymore. It's too exhausting. He might have hired someone else by now, but if not, would you mind working in San Diego instead of L.A.?" She filled two mugs with hot water and dunked tea bags, then handed one cup to Sera.

"Are you kidding? Of course I wouldn't mind." *The farther she was from Vancouver the better.*

"It'll be lots of responsibility and not much money. He's working on a shoestring—what else is new. But it'll be good on your résumé, and in my opinion you're more than ready to do a big project on your own. Look, I'll give him a call early in the morning. I'll tell him he's damned lucky if he gets you. He's a good guy, Pasquale. It's just him and me together that doesn't work."

"Thanks, Maisie." Tears threatened. "By rights you oughta just leave me in the lurch for walking out on you this way."

"If this was the beginning of filming instead of the end, I would." Maisie was matter-of-fact. "I wouldn't have any choice. I just wish you'd level with me about what's really going on with you. Yesterday the hunky doctor comes by the set, takes you out to lunch, everything looks like hearts and flowers. Today you're leaving." She sipped her tea, her blue eyes trained on Sera. "Does he know you're skipping town?"

Sera shook her head. She was going to be a coward about telling him. She'd leave a message on his machine. Or maybe she'd just fax him at the office.

"You never did get his apartment decorated. He could sue you for breach of promise."

Sera managed a wan smile. "I don't think there's much danger of that."

"So you're flying out sometime tomorrow?"

Sera nodded. "Tomorrow night. There's not much stuff to pack at the apartment. I'll say good-bye to my family and then catch the next flight." She got to her feet. "It's late. I'll let you go to bed."

Maisie saw her to the door and gave her a long hug. "This is ironic—you leaving Vancouver and me staying. I've made an offer on a town house on Richards Street. I should know by Monday whether I get it. If I do, it'll be the first place I've ever owned by myself."

"Maisie, that's wonderful. This is a great city to live in."

"But not for you."

Vancouver was home. It always hurt to leave it. It would always be home. "Not for me, no." Sera opened the door to leave, but Maisie put a hand on her arm.

"There's a saying, Buddhist or something, that you take yourself with you wherever you go. Sometimes running away doesn't solve anything, luv. If you want to come back, call me. We'll work something out about the job."

"Thanks, Maisie." Her generosity and kindness were overwhelming. "I don't think that'll happen, but I appreciate the offer.'' Sera didn't try to choke back the tears. ''You're such a good friend.''

''Good ones are the only kind worth having.'' But Maisie's banter didn't hide the fact that her eyes were as wet as Sera's. ''Godspeed, Cardano.''

BEN'S ENTIRE WEEK had been frantically busy, and Friday promised more of the same. He'd agreed to do a slide presentation for the nursing staff at St. Joe's at noon, but the surgery he'd scheduled for the morning had lasted much longer than anticipated. It was ten past twelve by the time he sprinted from the OR to the lecture room, buttoning on a clean shirt as he went.

The room was full. He strode to the podium, found his notes and began immediately, pleased that early in the day Dana had dropped off the materials he needed and they were waiting when he arrived.

He'd collected slides from some of his more interesting procedures, and after a short introduction in which he explained the difference between grafts and flaps for cosmetic reconstruction, he turned on the projector to illustrate the methods he and his colleagues used to correct the problems presented.

''This is a baby of eleven months whose head was run over by a car. Miraculously, there was no major brain injury, but the temporal bone was exposed here.'' He pointed.

"In a sense, plastic surgeons are a body scavenger, in that we find tissue from a nearby site—leaving the blood vessels attached, in this instance—and transfer it to the necessary area. We used a rotation flap from the donor site here." He indicated the baby's abdomen. "This is how baby looks now, six months after the surgery." The child appeared absolutely normal. He grinned at the camera, and the scar had all but vanished.

A murmur of approval and admiration came from the audience.

"This next patient is a thirty-two-year-old. The pile driver he was operating dropped on his foot, causing severe crush injuries. As you can see, damage to the soft tissue was extensive and the tendons were exposed. We used muscle from his thigh—" Ben pointed "—and grafted skin from the abdomen over the wound, thus avoiding amputation. The only problem is that this gentleman now has to shave his foot occasionally—the hair on the skin taken from the abdomen grows."

Everyone laughed.

Ben was relaxed. He enjoyed talking to an audience, and he knew from the warm response that he was doing a good job.

"Fifty percent of plastic surgery is artistic, fifty percent technical," he explained. "A good plastic surgeon can visualize the final result before he begins the procedure. The ideal situation is when you're able to take a physical problem and make it a nonissue.''

He clicked to the next slide, a photo of Gemma Cardano after her accident. ''For instance, this is a twenty-nine-year-old female who was struck in the face at a construction site by a two-by-four. She sustained a La Forte fracture, in which all the bones connecting the face to the skull were broken. Working through the nostrils and the soft palate, we reconstructed her face. We began by repairing the jaw right after the accident. The other operation took place eight days later.''

He switched to a photo of Gemma immediately postop, and then one shot earlier this week.

''The patient will be back to normal as soon as the swelling and bruising recede and we remove the wires from her jaw. This is her identical twin, whom we were able to use as a model for the computer imaging—a most unusual occurrence. We expect the patient's features to replicate hers once healing is completed.''

It pleased Ben to have Sera's face on the screen. It was almost as if, for a few moments, she was with him in the room. To look at her face gave him a warm, happy feeling.

He missed her so much it astonished him. He'd last seen her on Tuesday, when he'd visited the set of *Dinah* and taken her to lunch, and he'd intended to call the following day and take her somewhere nice for dinner, but he'd ended up working round the clock, instead. A huge fire had broken out in a downtown rooming house, and he'd spent untold hours treating burn patients. Then a child whose arm had been cut off in a farm accident was flown in, and the intricate procedure to reattach the limb required hours. An emergency with one of his own patients consumed another block of time, and he'd had more than the usual number of scheduled morning surgeries, as well as meetings in the evenings.

He'd even had to call on the dog-walking agency he used in times of dire emergency to feed and exercise Grendel.

He vowed to himself he'd phone Sera the moment this presentation was finished.

As soon as the question period was over he found a phone and dialed her cell number.

"The customer you are trying to reach is not available at this time."

He swore under his breath and called her apartment number, instead, marveling that he'd somehow committed both numbers to memory.

"The number you have reached is not in service."

Ben cursed the vagaries of the telephone company and redialed. The message was the same. There must be something wrong with the line.

It took fourteen minutes to reach a living person at the telephone company, and by that time he was both impatient and angry. He had patients waiting at his office, and inefficiency of this sort infuriated him.

"I'm sorry, sir," an operator told him, "that number is no longer in service. The subscriber notified us to stop service."

"That's ridiculous. That can't be. When exactly did she call you?"

"I'm sorry, sir. I can't release that information."

Ben slammed down the receiver.

It was a mistake. It had to be a mistake. Sera wouldn't just take off without telling him.

He hurried out of the hospital and across the street to his office, frantically trying to come up with a logical explanation. As he strode through the waiting room, he was barely aware of his patients. Dana said something as he passed her desk, but he didn't respond.

Inside the office, he glowered at the soft coffee-with-cream leather chairs Sera had picked out and tried to figure out what to do next.

Dana bustled in. "These are urgent phone messages, this is today's mail and these are faxes you haven't read yet. I'll send you your first patient in five minutes, all right, Doctor?"

He grunted, sorting through the messages and then the envelopes, searching for something from Sera, but there was nothing. He flipped through the faxes and there on the bottom was the one he was looking for:

Ben,
Sorry for not getting in touch with you in person. Something's come up and I'm going back to L.A. Sorry, also, for not getting the loft done as I promised. I enjoyed our time together, and thanks for all you've done for Gemma.

                                        Sera

He scowled at the terse wording. "Sorry for not getting in touch in person"? "Something's come up in L.A."? That was it?

What had possessed her to leave in such a hurry? And to say goodbye by fax was a slap in his face. A wave of absolute frustration and anger shot through him, and he used language he'd forgotten he knew. Viciously, he punched the button on the office intercom that would connect to Dana.

"Get Maisie Jones on the phone for me. She works on the set of *Dinah* over at False Creek Productions on West Second. Tell her it's urgent. As soon as she's on the line I want to speak to her."

Two patients later, Dana stuck her head in the door.

"Your caller is on line two, Doctor."

Ben excused himself and went into the inner office to take the call.

"Maisie? Ben Halsey here. Listen, what the hell's going on with Sera? I got this cryptic message saying she's gone back to L.A., and I'm worried about her."

He listened and then scowled at the receiver. "We didn't have a fight. We didn't even have an argument, for cripes sake. The last time I saw her was lunch on Tuesday, the day I came over to the set. Everything was fine then. What happened to make her run off this way?"

He listened again. Maisie was insisting she didn't know the reasons for Sera's departure any more than he did.

"Well, give me a phone number where I can reach her. I need to talk to her."

But Maisie refused, saying that if Sera wanted to get in touch with him, she'd do it on her own.

An overwhelming urge to holler at Maisie almost overcame him, but somehow he managed to be marginally polite as the conversation ended. Summoning up every ounce of self-discipline he could muster, Ben returned to his patient. The moment the consultation was over, he called Dana in.

"How many patients are out there waiting?"

"Two. Your one o'clock hasn't shown up yet."

"Phone all the afternoon patients and reschedule. I'll see whoever's here, but after that I'm taking the afternoon off.'' He'd never before felt that his office was a prison, but he did today.

"All right, Doctor." Dana looked concerned. "You aren't sick, I hope."

Ben snapped, "I'm just fine. Can't I take a couple of hours off without being sick?"

"I only asked, Doctor." Dana gave him an injured look and marched out.

Somehow, Ben made it through the next two patients. When the second one finally ambled out the door, he let out a sigh and picked up the phone, dialing the Brulottes' number and hoping against hope that Greg wasn't on shift at St. Joe's.

Here, at least, Ben's luck was good. Greg answered on the third ring, and he had no objections at all to Ben dropping by. Lily was having a massage; the nanny, Judith, was at an English class; and Stanley was sleeping.

"If you hurry, we can have a quiet beer before the kid wakes up."

Ben hurried. Much as he loved Stanley, he hoped he'd nap for the rest of the afternoon so there'd be a chance to talk to Greg uninterrupted.

Within half an hour, Ben was seated on the Brulottes' deck in the sunshine, but neither sun nor the cold beer at his elbow was helping his disposition.

"Why the hell would she do a thing like that, Greg? Just take off without so much as an explanation?"

Greg shrugged. "You got me. I'm no expert on female psychology."

"You oughta be. You're married," Ben said accusingly.

Greg laughed. "Spoken like a true bachelor. Any married guy'll tell you there isn't a man alive who really understands what goes on in a woman's mind. And that includes the male shrinks at St. Joe's."

"I've never had a woman I liked do this before, just turn her back and desert me."

Greg grinned without a trace of sympathy. "Tough on the old ego, huh?"

Was that all it was? Ben thought it over, trying his best to be objective.

"Some," he admitted grudgingly. There was more to it than that, though, and he struggled to pinpoint what it was.

"Something about Sera's different, and I really wanted to get to know her better."

Greg gave him an appraising look. "You in love with her, old buddy?"

"Of course not." The forceful denial was immediate, but Greg's questions had made him feel as if someone had punched him in the stomach, and after a moment Ben added, "How the hell do you ever know, anyway? How did you know with Lily?"

Greg locked his hands behind his head and

squinted up at the sky. "I was pretty thick about it. It took a while before I caught on. Then I figured I'd lost her, and that did it. You know, deep in your gut, when the right woman comes along. And you know you'd be a bloody fool to let her get away."

Ben thought that over and decided it wasn't very helpful. "I'm just not much good at this emotional-intimacy stuff," he finally blurted. "I'm better if it's just physical."

Greg eyed him quizzically. "That's not exactly late-breaking news, my friend." Greg knew about Vera, knew the reasons Ben kept relationships casual.

"The thing is, this wasn't."

Greg frowned. "Wasn't what?"

"Wasn't, uhhh, physical. Which is why I don't know why the hell I'm feeling this way."

"Feeling what way?"

"What're you doing—psychoanalyzing me?" The probing was starting to get under his skin. Ben scowled and finished off his beer, realizing he was being an asshole and not caring.

"Hell, no." Greg reached in the cooler he'd conveniently placed under the table and handed him another. "I'm trying to figure out why you're so ticked off. It's not the first time in your life you've gotten dumped. You say you're not in love with her, and you've just admitted you weren't even having sex with her, and you don't do the emotional stuff, which means there couldn't have been much of a connection, am I right?''

Ben refused to answer.

"By the way, Lily really liked Sera. She said, and I quote, 'It's about time you found yourself a grown-up lady.'''

Ben grunted. If Greg was trying to make him feel better, he wasn't doing much of a job of it. "It wasn't anything serious. I guess I just wanted some time to get to know her better," he finally concluded in a sulky tone.

"So, what's stopping you? It's Friday, which means you can take off if you want to, and the last I heard, there were still several flights a day heading south.''

Ben opened his mouth to protest and then thought it over. He couldn't remember what was scheduled for Monday, but at least the weekend was free.

"I don't know where the hell she is," he griped. "Her boss wouldn't tell me. I can't ask her parents. They'll be just like her boss, wondering why she didn't give me the address herself.''

"Where's your imagination, Halsey? You're not gonna let a little thing like an address stop you, are you?''

No, by God, he wasn't.

"Could you keep Grendel for me for a couple days?''

Having Stanley maul him would be hard on the dog, but it was for an excellent cause.

"Absolutely. Just drop him off on your way to the airport, Romeo." Greg was laughing at him again, but this time Ben didn't give a damn.

"Thanks for the beer. Gotta go. Tell my godson I'll bring him something from L.A."

CHAPTER TWELVE

THE CONSTRUCTION SITE beside St. Joe's was a hive of activity, but Aldo Cardano was nowhere to be found. Jack Kilgallin was operating a crane and Ben had to wait until he took a break and climbed down.

"Hello, Doc." Jack wiped his forehead with a rag and took a long swig from a water bottle. "What can I do for you?"

Ben had planned a dozen different openings on the way over. Now he scrapped all of them.

"I need to know where Sera Cardano is, and I thought maybe you could tell me." He met the other man's steady gaze and added, "I really need to talk to her. It's personal, and believe me, it's vitally important."

"Why not ask her parents? Or Gemma?"

"I came over here to find Aldo. But he's not around, and I don't have time to make a dozen phone calls."

"You in love with Sera, Doc?" It was the second time today someone had asked that, and for the second time, the words felt like a blow to Ben's midsection.

"I don't know." He wondered for an instant why he hadn't denied it outright again.

Jack studied him for what seemed like a minute. "Gemma told me Sera's in San Diego. She got a job she wants down there, and she had to leave right away to take it."

"Any idea where she is exactly? A phone number, an address?"

Ben's heart sank when Jack shook his head.

"All I remember is that the movie company's called Heartscape Productions, and the guy she's working for is named Pasquale something or other." Jack thought for a minute and then added, "Pasquale Young, that's it. The name sorta stuck in my head. Who'd imagine a big-time producer with a first name like Pasquale and a last name like Young?"

"Thanks, Jack. I owe you one."

Ben jogged across Burrard, hoping against hope that Dana would still be in the office. Conscientious soul that she was, she wouldn't have taken the afternoon off just because he had, would she? He could do this himself, but Dana would do it in half the time.

The outer office door was locked, but Dana was there, busily entering data onto the computer from a stack of files.

"Dana, thank God you're still here."

She raised her eyebrows at him as he blurted out,

"I need you to locate a man named Pasquale Young. He works for Heartscape Productions in San Diego. It's a movie company. Tell whoever you talk to that I have to speak to him immediately. It's a medical emergency."

He hurried into the inner office and dialed the airline. There were no direct flights to San Diego, but a flight was leaving Vancouver at seven that evening for Los Angeles. Which would mean a long wait if he wanted to a connection to San Diego. Ben booked a seat anyhow. He could rent a car at the airport and drive to San Diego in a couple of hours.

He still didn't know where Sera was. He went to see how Dana was making out. She had the phone pressed to her ear. "I talked to several assistants. They gave me a cell number. I'm trying that now— Hello, Mr. Young?" Dana repeated what Ben had told her and then handed over the phone.

"Dr. Ben Halsey calling, Mr. Young, from Vancouver, Canada." Ben dredged up an officious tone, ignoring Dana's amused expression. "It's imperative that I get in touch with Sera Cardano immediately. I'm her sister's physician. Do you have a phone number or address where Ms. Cardano can be reached?"

Pasquale Young was a trusting soul. In another few moments, Ben had the name of a motel.

SERA FINISHED folding the laundry and slumped onto the bed, miserably aware that the tank top she was wearing smelled of perspiration and her shorts were crumpled and grimy. She'd had to wait for a washer, and then wait again for a dryer at the Laundromat down the street, and she felt grubby and utterly exhausted.

Outside, the midsummer air was thick, hot and unbearably muggy, in spite of the fact that the ocean was only a short distance away. The motel room was supposed to be air-conditioned, but the machine in the window wasn't doing its job.

She should shower and go to bed. It was almost midnight and tomorrow morning she had to get up early and go looking for a furnished apartment. This place wasn't bad. She'd chosen it because it was close to the beach, but she needed something more permanent, even if it meant living some distance from the water. When he'd hired her today, Pasquale had told her they'd be here several months at least.

Maybe when she got settled in a more permanent place, she'd start feeling better. This blackness that seemed to weigh her down was probably just a reaction to being in a strange city where she didn't yet know anyone, she tried to tell herself.

The other members of the crew had been friendly when Pasquale introduced them, but it was too soon to hope they'd invite her to join them for a pizza and a beer.

She should be thankful she'd gotten a job this fast, and she was; she'd sent Maisie a cute card that afternoon, expressing her love and her gratitude. But grateful or not, she still felt like crying most of the time. She'd never been this alone or utterly miserable in her life, and she couldn't stop thinking of Ben.

The knock at the door scared her. She sprang to her feet and stood immobile, heart hammering, head spinning from her having jumped up so fast.

"Sera? Sera, it's me, Ben."

Ben? *Ben?* It couldn't be. A sense of unreality came over her, and she wondered if she was about to faint.

At last she staggered over and opened the door, and stared at him, speechless.

"Can I come in?" He sounded amused. "It's hot and muggy out here. I'd forgotten San Diego is almost Mexico."

"What—" She stopped and cleared her throat. "Ben. What—what are you doing here?" She stepped aside to let him in and then shut the door.

"I wanted to take you out to dinner," he said as if that explained everything. "I guess it's too late for that. Maybe we could find a place to have a cool drink, instead?"

"You—you came all the way to San Diego to

take me out to dinner?'' She stared at him, dumb-founded. ''What—what about Gemma?''

''Gemma?'' He looked bewildered. ''What about her? She's doing fine. She has another appointment next week.''

''You—you don't think this is unfair, leaving her…?''

''Of course not.'' He was genuinely puzzled. ''She's just fine, Sera. And I have an excellent man covering for me. If something should go wrong he's more than capable of dealing with it. I certainly don't anticipate any problems with your sister.''

Unless he was a consummate liar, he really didn't know what she meant. The weight inside Sera's heart eased somewhat. He seemed to view Gemma only as his patient. Had her sister gotten it all wrong, then? Had she misinterpreted his profes-sional attention as personal?

It was possible. Thinking it over, Sera suddenly realized that was more than possible. Gemma had been seriously injured. She wasn't back to normal; she wasn't thinking straight. And Ben was here. She, Sera, wasn't his patient. He'd come all this way— Could he have come all this way solely to see her?

''Are you here on a conference or something, Ben?''

''Nope. I just wanted to see you.''

Her heart expanded, and all of a sudden she

thought about how she looked—and probably smelled.

He was moving toward her, as if he was about to take her in his arms, and she panicked.

"I was just going to have a shower. I'm really sweaty. It's so hot. I had to do the laundry. I was going to go to bed." She drew in a deep breath and blew it out again. "I still don't get this, Ben."

"It's not difficult. I needed to see you, Sera. I felt we were friends, and that fax was a shock. I wasn't ready to say goodbye like that. I wasn't ready to say goodbye at all."

There it was. The last of the heaviness drifted away like smoke, and for the first time in days she felt like smiling.

"But—where are you staying?"

"Here."

She must have appeared shocked, because he shook his head and laughed, adding, "In this motel, I meant. Even I wouldn't have been so presumptuous. I'm in unit 237."

"How did you get here?" She knew she sounded stupid. She couldn't seem to make her brain work properly.

"I flew to L.A. and rented a car."

"But how did you find me?"

"I talked to Mr. Young."

"You talked to Pasquale?"

He looked slightly abashed. "I'll explain everything if you'll come out for a drink. And maybe a burger or something. I'm starving. They don't exactly give you a lot to eat on that plane.''

''I need to shower.''

''Sure, okay, I'll go and get settled and come back for you in what, ten minutes?''

It was ten to twelve. What was she doing, going out with him at nearly midnight?

''Twenty.''

She was ready in fifteen.

He tapped at the door just as she was sliding bare feet into sandals.

He'd changed into khaki shorts and a blue cotton shirt. He, too, had taken a quick shower. He looked unbearably handsome.

''How beautiful you are in that dress, Sera.''

It was a simple pink cotton shift that ended midthigh. Suddenly, she felt beautiful.

He escorted her out to his rented car.

''What did you do with Grendel?''

''He's having a sleepover with the Brulottes.''

She thought of Stanley and laughed. ''Poor Grendel.''

''He'll survive. It's like doggie boot camp. It'll toughen him up, give him character.''

She'd forgotten how easily Ben could make her laugh.

They ended up at a fast-food chain, eating burgers and drinking iced tea. She was finishing the last bite of her fries when he said, "Okay, Sera Cardano. Now, explain why you left the way you did. I thought we were friends."

Should she tell him about Gemma, what Gemma believed about herself and Ben?

She couldn't. It would be a betrayal of her sister's confidence. "I told you my career comes first," she improvised. "Because of Maisie, I had this wonderful opportunity to do the sets for a 1920s miniseries. I couldn't pass it up."

"But you said you were going back to L.A. You didn't even mention San Diego."

Liars needed good memories, her mama had always said. Maria was right about something else, too. One lie always led to another.

"They changed the venue at the last minute."

He was watching her, and when he slowly nodded it was a relief. He believed her, and he didn't belabor the issue.

Instead, he reached across and took her hand in his, stroking her fingers in a way that sent shivers up her spine.

"We have two whole days, Ms. Career Lady. I fly back first thing Monday morning. Would you spend forty-eight hours exploring San Diego with me?"

For one instant, she thought again of Gemma. But her sister was far away, and Ben was here of his own free will, and forty-eight hours together sounded like bliss. "I'd love that. Have you been to San Diego before?"

"Once, but I was heading for Mexico, so I didn't have a chance to see much. We'll drive around tomorrow, I have a map and a tourist brochure that came with the rental car."

Sera glanced at her watch. "If we're going to get any sleep, we'd better go back to the motel."

They drove along quiet streets, with the car radio playing classical music. Sera dared to pretend they were just a couple of tourists returning to their motel after an evening spent dining and dancing.

Ben walked her to the door of her unit.

"'Night, Sera." He drew her to him and kissed her, lightly but passionately. "See you in the morning for breakfast about what, nine? Ten?"

"Nine." She didn't intend to waste one precious moment, and by his pleased smile she knew he felt the same.

He ran his palm down her cheek, and impulsively she pressed her lips there before she turned, suddenly shy, and went inside.

She should have been too excited to sleep, but she closed her eyes and the next thing she knew it was 8:15 and outside her window the California sun was beginning to burn off the early-morning sea mist.

Ben was punctual to the minute. She opened the door to his knock and there he stood, smiling at her, looking so handsome and familiar and happy she couldn't help but smile back.

If faces could ache from smiling, hers would have that entire glorious day. They drove and walked and explored and ate, everywhere from Balboa Park and the zoo to the sleek racing yachts being built on Shelter Island. They talked all day, and by evening it seemed to Sera she had a zillion more things to tell him, and as many to hear about him.

In the hot summer twilight, he drove her to Old Town for a Mexican dinner. They chose an outdoor restaurant festooned with paper lanterns and fresh flowers. The air smelled of barbecue and baking beans. Ben ordered traditional margaritas.

"*¿Grande?*" the lovely Spanish waitress asked, her dark eyes twinkling.

"*Mucho grande,*" Ben replied, and when the drinks arrived Sera gasped. The stemmed glasses were the size of fishbowls.

"I can't possibly drink all that, Ben." But when she sipped experimentally, the icy concoction tasted wonderful.

The food arrived, platters of rice and beans and spicy vegetables and chilled salads. A mariachi band played. A dark and handsome man with a thrilling tenor voice serenaded her, and Ben pretended to be jealous. A flower vendor stopped by and Ben bought a fresh white gardenia and came around the table to thread the stem through her hair so the flower sat just above her ear. He slid his fingers under the spill of her heavy hair and touched her nape with his fingertips, and she shivered. Spanish words and lighthearted laughter rose and fell all around her.

Sera relished every drop of her margarita.

Pleasantly dizzy and more than a little tipsy, she hung on Ben's arm as they walked to a tiny historic theater to watch a play. She sat beside him in the dimly lit room, laughing at the hilarious lines but aware mostly of her palm pressed against his.

And every moment, she felt that a part of her was observing, nodding in satisfaction and saying, *So* this *is how it feels to be carefree and young. This is how it feels to be with someone you might come to love.*

After the play, he insisted on buying her a magnificent scarlet-and-black Mexican shawl to tie over a bathing suit or use as a wrap on a summer evening. And during the drive back to the motel, he turned the radio to a Spanish country-and-western station and sang along, making up his own fractured and funny versions of the maudlin songs. He kept her hand locked inside his fingers, resting on the hard muscles of his thigh, his thumb stroking across her skin.

She closed her eyes and rested her head against the back of the seat. She was happier than she could remember being since she was a child. She felt pampered and cherished and admired.

She wanted the night never to end, but she knew that when it inevitably did, she wanted it to be in Ben's arms.

She didn't want to sleep alone tonight.

CHAPTER THIRTEEN

BEN PULLED into the motel lot and turned off the motor.

Sera had been debating what to say once they arrived, and now she made up her mind.

"Would you like to come in for coffee?" It was such a clumsy way to do it, but it was the only way she could think of at the moment. She wanted to just say, *Would you like to come in and make love with me?* But men liked to make the first move, she still believed, in spite of the sexes being equal. And what if he refused? She'd feel such a fool.

She held her breath. What if she'd guessed wrong? What if...

"Sounds good."

She breathed again.

They reached her door, and she fished out the key and, on the third try, fumbled it into the lock.

"Let me." The door opened smoothly and he followed her inside.

She headed to the minuscule kitchen, where she plugged in the kettle and poked in her cupboard for the jar of instant coffee. She was so nervous as she put it in the cups that she spilled granules across the counter. "Cream and sugar?"

"Black is fine."

When the coffee was finally ready he took his cup and sat on the sofa, patting the seat beside him. She sat down facing him, cradling her cup between her palms the way she longed to cradle his face. Their eyes met, and she saw reflected a silent acknowledgment of raw physical desire. She'd been right. Ben felt it, too.

His eyes were caressing her, and her skin prickled. She was burning up. She looked away, searching for something to say that would deflect the tension.

"I think I got too much sun today," she blurted.

Fantastic, Cardano. Now he knows that just sitting beside him makes you hot. So much for being subtle.

He didn't answer. Instead, he set down his coffee, took hers and put it down, as well. Then he slid an arm around her shoulders and moved over beside her, his body not quite touching hers, but almost.

"I want you, Sera." His voice was no more than an urgent, husky whisper. "I don't want to rush you, but I ache with wanting you."

She knew how that felt. She'd been aching herself. All day. Longer. Probably ever since the first time he'd kissed her that first night in his apartment in Gastown.

Right now, she badly wanted him to kiss her again. What was he waiting for? She tilted her head up and touched his lips with hers ever so lightly, inviting him.

His breath rasped in her ear, and he pulled her into his arms. "Careful, sweetheart. This could get dangerous." His voice was rough and not quite steady. "Are you sure it's what you want, Sera?"

She thought he was telling her again that sex was as much as he had to give. There'd be no future with him. There'd be passion and laughter and excitement, but the time would come, perhaps very soon, when it would all be over.

Was that what she wanted? Was she ready to take the chance that her heart would stay intact if they continued?

Her brain had misgivings, but her body did its best to overrule them. She had needs like every other woman, she reasoned. Was it so wrong to give in to them, to grab at the pleasure she desired without worrying over the aftermath?

"I'm sure, Ben."

Having sex with someone like Halsey is like playing with nitroglycerin. Maisie's cautionary words came back to her, but she pushed them away. Men's and women's needs weren't really that different, were they?

There was also the element of trust. Strange as it seemed, she now trusted Ben. The conversation they'd had about Gemma last night when he arrived, even some casual remarks he'd made today, had absolutely convinced her he had no feelings for her sister except those of a concerned physician for a patient.

"Are you always this slow at the beginning?" She kept her tone light, but there was a nervous catch in her voice.

The next thing she knew, he'd lifted her in his arms and they were heading for the bedroom.

Sera gave a squawk of alarm and wrapped her arms around his neck.

"Put me down, you maniac." She'd watched muscle men on California beaches pick up their bimbos and run toward the water. She'd watched movie heroes swing their slender leading ladies into their arms and climb staircases. She'd always been certain those scenes were executed by stuntmen. Once or twice she'd idly wondered how it would feel to be carried in a man's arms. Now that it was happening to her, she could only think of how much she weighed and whether Ben's back would give out.

He was maneuvering them through the narrow bedroom door much the way stagehands carefully moved large pieces of furniture through small openings, and her legs got caught. The scene was becoming so ludicrous Sera started to giggle help-lessly.

"So you find my romantic impulses funny, do you?" They'd reached the bed. He dumped her un-ceremoniously and then collapsed beside her, pre-tending to be out of breath.

"There goes my libido," he moaned in a pathetic voice.

Sera laughed until she was giddy.

"Now, you disrespectful woman, where was I?" In one sudden lithe movement, he rolled over and trapped her beneath him, his thighs on either side of her legs, his hands by her shoulders, bracing himself so he wouldn't crush her. He took his glasses off and tossed them on the bedside table.

Bending forward, he kissed her, light, flickering kisses at first, kisses that made her hungry for more.

She squirmed impatiently and at last his kiss deepened, devouring her, his tongue promising a rhythm she longed for.

He drew back and brushed a lock of hair away from her face, and she looped both hands around his neck and tugged him down again, using her mouth to convey the feverish anticipation that burned inside her.

"Too many clothes." He caught the hem of her dress and maneuvered it up and over her head in one easy movement.

"You, too." His polo shirt was tucked into the

waistband of his cotton pants, and she struggled to pull it out. At last she tugged it loose, and he took over, stripping off the shirt in one deft motion.

"Hurry. Please, Ben." She wanted his hands all over her. She wanted his skin against hers. She wanted him inside her. She'd never wanted anything as much, or as impatiently.

Her bra fastened in front and he unsnapped it, leaning forward to draw one firm nipple greedily into his mouth, his breath rapid and fiery hot against her bare, tender skin. She bucked and whimpered, as he trailed his hand up her inner thigh, strong fingers brushing the silky crotch of her panties, making her breath catch in a sob of longing.

"You feel so good," he said, stroking, circling, slipping his finger under the fabric and inside her, withdrawing when she surged against him, touching and retreating in a clever dance that nearly drove her mad. "You are so sexy, my beautiful Sera."

Was she really his? For now, for this moment. And this moment was all there was.

She fumbled to unfasten the button and zipper on his pants, then reached inside to hold him, to give him back some of the pleasure he was lavishing on her. He was hard and hot in her hand.

"Careful," he groaned, but it was a long moment before he drew away, and then it was only to strip off his pants and underwear.

She looked at him and found him utterly beautiful.

His abdomen was flat, his erection rising from the mass of dark curls. The same curls covered his chest and dusted his muscular arms and legs.

She wanted him.

Ben cradled her head between his palms and brought his face close to hers. "Concentrate," he whispered. "Concentrate only on this."

He rubbed himself against her, slipping between her thighs, using the silken barrier of her panties to tantalize them both.

"And this."

He took her mouth and tongue in a kiss that was savage and slow, and then he gripped the elastic of her panties and drew them down her thighs.

All she was conscious of was hunger, raw and demanding, and she used her legs to frantically work the panties off. She kicked them away and then tilted her pelvis high, wordlessly inviting.

In the madness of desire she'd forgotten about protection, but he hadn't. He reached into the pocket of the pants he'd placed conveniently near, withdrew a condom, rolled it into place, and a second later nestled between her thighs. He touched her with his fingers, and then tasted her with his mouth, drawing, sucking, driving her close to the edge, making her gasp for breath and cry out.

At last, at last, he slid inside, and she sobbed with

gratitude. As he began to move, she matched him. But soon her convulsions began deep inside and she gave herself up to them, burying her face in his neck, mindless and shuddering with pleasure.

An instant later he joined her, his cry of pleasure as ecstatic and lost to the world as hers had been.

When at last thoughts formed again for Sera, only one was clear and definite and greedy: *She wanted more. She wanted as much lovemaking as they could manage, tonight, tomorrow, tomorrow night.* She wouldn't think beyond that. She'd make each moment count. She'd make all those moments enough for the time when he'd be gone.

HE PULLED the sheet back up over them and tucked them beneath the light blanket, curling her pliant naked body close to his. She sighed, one long, deep, trembling sigh. He felt her relax fully and slide into sleep. After a few moments she snored lightly, and he smiled. He wouldn't tell her she snored. It would be his secret, intimate and very personal and dear.

He thought of Greg, and sent heartfelt thanks through the ether for putting the idea for this trip in his head. Today had been extraordinary, filled with laughter and great conversation, with that constant undercurrent of pure sexual energy.

And the lovemaking had been... He searched for a superlative and couldn't find one. There'd been rightness about making love to Sera, a sense of deep partnering that was unique in his experience.

Or maybe it was just because it was new and fresh. Certainly Sera was a lovely, passionate woman, but he would be making a mistake to start reading more into this than there was.

They would have to carry on a long-distance relationship, he reminded himself, and that could cause problems. He'd tried it once or twice, and it hadn't worked well; one or the other had gotten tired of never having someone around to go out with on a last-minute casual date.

But Sera was like him in many ways, totally dedicated to her career, not looking for anything long-term, so their relationship probably wouldn't last beyond a couple of months. Now, why wasn't that as comforting as it used to be?

He dismissed the thought.

This would work for as long as it worked, but at this moment the trip home was something he didn't want to think about.

There was still tomorrow to enjoy. He'd talked to the waitress at the restaurant when he'd paid the bill, and she'd suggested driving over the border into Mexico—Tijuana was only a half hour away. She'd given him directions to a seafood dine-and-dance spot the locals favored, twenty or thirty miles down the Pacific Coast.

He hadn't told Sera yet; it would be a surprise

for the morning. He loved the way her expressive face registered excitement and pleasure. He loved her enthusiasm, her quick wit, her absolute honesty.

Are you in love with her? The question popped into his head, and he firmly tossed it out again, telling himself that if he ever did fall in love with a woman, she'd be someone like Sera.

He pressed his lips against her shoulder and surrendered to sleep.

MONDAY'S MAIL brought another envelope, and Gemma eagerly ripped it open.

Gemma,
I've come to know your body,
Intimately,
Not from making love
But from memorizing
The way you move
A shoulder, an eyelash.
I know your touch,
Not from your skin on mine,
No.
Instead I watch you thread
Your fingers through your hair,
Or slide your tongue across your lips.
Once I watched you sleep,
And whispered what I wanted you to hear
But you were far away and didn't listen.

> Still, sometimes you smile at me
> And caress me with your eyes,
> And it's enough.
> For now,
> Gemma.
> (It has to be.)

She read it over and over. As always, the poetry touched a deep and vulnerable place inside her, but today an overwhelming sense of guilt accompanied the pleasure.

She'd kissed Jack Saturday night. More than kissed him.

He'd started it. She'd been in a rotten mood all day. She missed Sera; she couldn't understand why her sister had insisted on taking that stupid job in San Diego.

When Jack had arrived in the evening she was foul, scrawling sarcastic comments on her pad and shoving them at him.

Aldo and Maria had gone to a movie, and afterward they were having dinner with relatives, so they wouldn't be back until late.

Jack opened the wine he'd brought and offered Gemma a glass with a straw, unperturbed by her bad temper. He'd laughed at her sniping and teased her out of it. They'd had more wine, and he'd somehow dared her into trying to kiss him with her jaw wired shut.

At first she'd just wanted to see if it was possible. They'd finished the wine, and they'd laughed a lot because the kissing part had been fun but not too successful.

Her face flamed when she remembered what followed, however. Jack was much too good with his mouth and hands, and there was that basic animal attraction that had always sparked between them. He'd kissed and touched other places besides her mouth, and she'd gotten carried away.

He hadn't; she'd learned a lot about Jack Kilgallin that night. He was a masterful lover, even without actual sexual contact, and he intuitively knew what would give her the most pleasure. He was controlled and proficient at making her feel safe while giving her license to go wild.

She'd just had too much wine, she told herself, and then admitted that was no excuse. How could she let body hunger get the best of her, when Ben was telling her so plainly he was willing to wait?

She was a cheat, she thought with disgust. She had no moral fortitude at all. She didn't deserve Ben. She'd never let Jack near her again.

When she'd finally come to her senses, she'd told him she never wanted to see him again.

He'd laughed, thinking she was joking. It had taken a lot of notes to convince him she meant it. And he'd lost his temper with her finally, which was a good thing because at least that ended it.

"You're nothing but an immature, selfish kid," he'd raged at her. There was nothing wrong with his vocabulary when he got mad, she noticed. "I kept thinking you'd grow up, but you're working hard at staying foolish. Well, Gemma, you don't have to worry about me bothering you again, because I'm out of here. I can put up with almost anything except stupidity." He'd stormed off, and for a while afterward she'd had trouble breathing, as if there wasn't enough air.

She'd also felt an incredible sense of loss, and when she finally got to sleep that night, she'd had erotic dreams, not about Ben but about Jack. When she woke up, she was crying. And part of her had waited all day Sunday for him to call or drop by, as if nothing had happened.

He didn't.

How could she be falling in love with one man and still long to do hot, intimate things with another? Gemma reasoned that she'd probably fooled around with Jack because the only connection she had to Ben was through the poems he sent her.

She needed to hear Ben admit that he cared for her, she decided, which she figured he'd never do as long as she was still his patient. But there were only three weeks left before the wires came out of her jaw. The swelling had pretty much disappeared, and it was obvious even to her that her face looked almost exactly as it had before. But three weeks felt like forever.

She had another appointment with Ben a week from this Wednesday. He'd told her it would be the last time he'd need to see her until her jaw healed.

She'd write him a letter, Gemma decided, and give it to him then. She'd let him know how much the poetry meant to her. She'd assure him she felt the same about him as he did about her. He didn't have to say anything; she'd know how he felt by the expression on his face when he read the letter, and by that time it would only be two weeks until her jaw was healed, hardly any time at all.

She desperately needed something more than poetry from him.

CHAPTER FOURTEEN

IT HAD BEEN a week and a half since San Diego, and Ben was having to dredge up an enormous amount of self-discipline to apply himself to his work instead of thinking about Sera—a state of affairs that was disturbing him a lot.

He'd arrived back Monday at noon, and come straight to the office from the airport, his mind on Sera and the weekend they'd spent together.

He'd kissed her goodbye at the motel very early that morning. She'd wanted to drive to the airport with him, but the logistics didn't make sense. He had to return the rental car, which would mean taking two vehicles to the airport.

Convincing her to spend every last instant they had together making love with him instead of driving back and forth to airports hadn't been difficult. He wanted to remember her in his bed, he insisted.

He'd dragged himself out of her arms and into the shower with barely enough time to make his flight, and even now, nine days later, in his mind's eye he could still see her, sweetly disheveled, her luxuriant hair spread in sexy disarray across the pillow they'd shared, her lips and breasts swollen and rosy from his mouth.

That memory hadn't faded as it ought to have in nine days. Which made it difficult right now to pay attention to Mrs. Newcombe, who thought one of her augmented breasts was noticeably larger than the other. It wasn't, but Mrs. Newcombe wasn't running on reason. She'd come to Ben for a second opinion; her surgeon was a man who did procedures on individuals Ben might have decided to refuse, and this was one of them.

The lady was obviously unhappy with her life, and nothing surgical would change that sad fact. Ben talked to her for over an hour, gently asserting again and again that another surgical procedure wasn't the answer.

In spite of his patience, Mrs. Newcombe left in a huff, and Ben sighed with relief when the office door closed behind her. It was almost lunchtime. He relaxed for a few moments before he buzzed Dana to send in his next patient, remembering the conversation he'd had on the telephone with Sera the night before.

They'd talked for over an hour, as they'd fallen in the habit of doing every night, discussing novels they were reading, plays and movies they wanted to see, music they'd heard and liked.

Ben had brought home the photos he'd taken of her before Gemma's operation. He'd pinned them up on the wall facing his bed so he could see different angles of her face as they spoke. He'd caught her smiling and frowning and laughing outright. The photos were a poor substitute for having her there beside him, but he was glad to have them nonetheless.

He enjoyed her outrageous vignettes about working with the passionate but quirky Pasquale.

In turn, Ben told her about Grendel, who'd insisted on sleeping on Ben's bed ever since his weekend with the Brulottes. He waited until Ben was asleep to crawl up on the bed, where he positioned himself carefully, head on the spare pillow, paws on Ben's back.

The dog was traumatized, Ben told Sera. He was checking into psychiatric help for him.

He liked to hear her laughter, full throated and hearty.

He glanced at the patient roster Dana had given him that morning, and was delighted to find that Gemma Cardano was next. Because of his relationship with Sera, he had a special tenderness for her sister, and he looked forward to seeing her, although he didn't fully understand the promise Sera had extracted from him before he left San Diego.

"Don't mention to Gemma that you were down here, or that you and I are seeing each other," she'd insisted. "I want to tell her myself when I come home."

It was probably a twin thing, he thought now. Whatever the reason, he certainly intended to honor the request.

He smiled at Gemma when she came in, scanning her features and feeling satisfied at the visible evidence of a job well done.

"This looks really good," he told her, taking her elbow, escorting her to the chair opposite his own. "Obviously you're healing really well. It's not going to be long now before your jaw's mended, and then your life can get completely back to normal."

He studied her. It was uncanny how very much she resembled Sera, but for him the similarity ended with their physical appearance. And the differences between them grew more apparent the longer he knew Sera.

There were subtle but important contrasts in their personalities. Gemma often had a petulance about her that was foreign to Sera. At first, he'd thought it was simply due to the accident, but he came to realize it was part of Gemma's basic character.

Sera had a temper, all right; he'd witnessed it several times. She exploded, said what she had to say and it was over, as quick and furious as a summer storm.

With Gemma, however, anger seemed to go deeper and last longer. In the hospital, he'd witnessed her being outright rude and obnoxious to Jack Kilgallin, with no apparent cause. Kilgallin dealt with it well; the man clearly worshiped Gemma. Ben had come to like and respect Jack; he was quiet and steady, but strong, the exact type of man, Ben surmised, who'd accept Gemma's quixotic moods with equanimity without allowing her to ride roughshod over him.

Ben kept up a steady stream of light conversation as he did his examination, bending over her, aware the whole time of Gemma's huge brown eyes, so like Sera's, watching his every move.

Being with Gemma made him achingly lonely for Sera. The intensity of that loneliness was unsettling; he didn't want to feel this strongly about anyone. He never had before.

"You're doing wonderfully well, Gemma," he said when the examination was done. "You're soon going to be as beautiful as—" He'd come very close to saying Sera. He quickly substituted "as you always were."

It touched him to see tears fill her eyes and trickle down her cheeks. He put a comforting hand on her shoulder, and to his shock and dismay, she instantly threw herself at him, wrapping her arms around his neck, pressing her body against him in an overtly sexual way.

Having a patient make a pass was a physician's worst nightmare. It could so easily be mishandled, resulting in nasty allegations of sexual misconduct, and the appalling part here was this was Sera's sister.

As gently as possible, Ben unhooked her arms and moved away a discreet distance. He plucked a handful of tissues from the box on the table and handed them to her when she fumbled in her purse, but tissues weren't what she was looking for.

She pulled out a folded paper and thrust it at him.

Ben unfolded it, and as he read quickly through it, horror and disbelief overwhelmed him. Certain phrases reverberated like bombshells in his brain.

...know how much you want to make your feelings for me clear, but I understand...

...I feel the same... Can't wait until you're no longer just my doctor...never loved anyone this much before...

Ben stared down at the paper, feeling sick, racking his brain for something to say that wouldn't hurt her, but would make his position absolutely clear in a way impossible for her to misconstrue.

"Gemma, sit down, please. We have to talk about this."

Panicked, he considered calling Dana in to witness what he was about to say. In other circumstances, he would have, but Dana's presence would embarrass Gemma even further, and for Sera's sake he couldn't bring himself to do so.

What could he tell Gemma that would make her understand how preposterous all this was? The only thing he could think of was to tell her about him and Sera.

There was no other way to handle this except with the absolute truth. He took a deep breath and prayed for inspiration, for some way of saying what he had to without humiliating Gemma more than necessary.

"Somehow I've given you the wrong impression of me," he began. This was awful, but he had no choice except to go on. "However it happened, I humbly apologize."

She was looking at him as if she were in a daze, as if she couldn't take in his words, so he tried again, more forcefully this time.

"Gemma, I never intended to mislead you in any way. I'm your doctor, nothing more.

"The fact is, I've been dating Sera. We're—we're—um, we're somewhat romantically involved. I visited her in San Diego. Sera wanted to tell you herself, but I felt you needed to know now, so you understand completely that I had no intention whatsoever of misleading *you*."

He watched Gemma's features register shock and disbelief and then, inevitably, embarrassment.

He felt deep compassion for her. She couldn't talk; could only react by scribbling a response on the pad he'd placed in front of her. That had to be impossibly difficult in a situation like this.

She scribbled, scratched it out with a violent motion, wrote something else. Her cheeks were crimson, her breathing stertorous. Her hand was shaking visibly, and when she shoved the pad at him, her eyes were wild. He felt a stab of apprehension. His uneasiness grew as he read what she'd scrawled.

"Poems?" He frowned and shook his head. "Sorry, Gemma, you've lost me here. I don't have any idea what you're talking about. What poems?"

A terrible sound came from her. It would have been a scream had she been able to open her mouth. She lurched to her feet. Swung at him, her fist connecting hard with his jaw. She was still making that desperate, awful noise. He reeled back, caught unprepared. Now she bent to the table and grabbed a handful of magazines. Her aim was good; the magazines connected, hitting him in the chest.

Only because of his quick reflexes was he able to dodge the potted plant she flung next. It crashed against the wall and sent dirt and fragments of broken pottery flying everywhere.

She was looking around for something else to throw.

Ben held his hands up and raised his voice. "That's enough, Gemma. Just calm down." But she ran at him, lashing out with her fists, pummeling his chest and trying to scratch his face.

In desperation, Ben dodged and took hold of her from behind, pinning her arms and doing his best to keep her from doing any more harm. Kicking and thrashing, butting at him with her head, she went on keening. Ben felt incredible relief when the door burst open and Dana said, "Doctor, what on earth is going on— Oh, my gosh, I'll call Security."

"No." Ben was puffing. "No, we can handle this." Gemma was very strong. For the next few moments, with Dana helping, Ben attempted to verbally calm Gemma. To no avail. She was sobbing now, still struggling fiercely as he held her. He was trying to prevent her from throwing anything else or attacking him again, but he was also concerned that she might choke. With her jaw wired, that could be very dangerous.

He told her so repeatedly, adding, "If you don't calm down, Gemma, I'm going to have to sedate you."

She ignored him and went on struggling.

"Get me Ativan 4, IM," he finally gasped to Dana.

The nurse brought in the syringe and, with Ben holding Gemma as still as possible, injected the tranquilizer into Gemma's arm. Within a few moments, Gemma quieted a little, still sobbing but not struggling anymore. Ben eased her into a chair, and Dana brought her a glass of water with a straw.

Gemma knocked the glass aside and the water sprayed over Dana. The glass shattered against the wall.

"There's no need for this sort of behavior." Dana was soaked and losing her patience. "We only want to help you, Ms. Cardano."

Ben was trying to figure out what to do next. Obviously, Gemma had to have someone to care for her. The sedative would put her to sleep shortly.

"Did you drive yourself here, Gemma?"

The drug was taking effect now. She nodded, motioning for a pencil and paper. Dana handed her both.

I want my father she printed with an unsteady hand, adding a phone number.

Ben made the call, and Aldo Cardano answered at once. The number had obviously been to his cell phone, because Ben could hear hammering and heavy equipment operating in the background.

"Gemma's here in my office, Aldo, and she's very upset. I've given her a sedative and she needs to be driven home," Ben said, grateful that Aldo didn't ask questions.

He arrived in minutes, wearing a hard hat and coveralls and a worried expression. He glanced around the room, at the broken pottery, the dirt spread across the carpet, the shattered glass.

"What the hell's going on here?" Without waiting for an answer, he held out his arms to his daughter. "Come here, *bambina.*"

Gemma got up and wobbled toward him. He

wrapped a protective arm around her shoulder. She was already very unsteady on her feet.

"What's this all about, Doctor? What's happened to her? Is she hurt?" Aldo gave Ben an accusing look. "Seems to me there's been one hell of a fight here."

"Physically she's fine. And no fight, just a misunderstanding." Ben felt this was not the time or place to go into details. "We were talking and she became hysterical. I've given her a strong sedative and she needs to go home and rest now. Perhaps you could call me later this afternoon, and I'll explain."

"You bet I will. I don't much like the looks of this." He glared at Ben and then turned his attention to Gemma. "C'mon, *cara*. Don't worry about your car. I'll get one of the guys to bring it home a little later."

He escorted her out of the office without another word.

CHAPTER FIFTEEN

BEN GRABBED a garbage can and knelt on the rug to clean up the mess, shaken by what had occurred and hardly able to believe things could have gotten out of control so quickly and with so little warning.

"What the heck happened, Doctor?" Dana brought in a broom and dustpan and began sweeping up debris from the rug.

Ben shook his head. "I wish I knew. Somehow she got the wrong impression. She thought that I...that is, she figured I..."

"She got it in her head that she was in love with you?"

"Something like that."

"Well, it's not the first time." There had been a patient, several years before. Ben had recognized what was happening and had made certain Dana was in the room during every visit. The woman had been sad, but certainly not violent. And he hadn't been involved with her sister.

"Ms. Cardano's a very pretty lady, probably used to getting what she wants," Dana commented. "She sure has a foul temper. Lucky she didn't hit you with that plant. I'll have to get the janitor in here with the vacuum. Good thing she was the last patient this morning. Nobody but me out there when the noise started.''

She dumped the contents of the dustpan into the wastebasket. ''You look pretty shaken up, Doctor. Why don't you go out and have some lunch. I'll get this cleaned up before the afternoon appointments.''

''Thanks, Dana.'' He did need to get out, although the thought of food wasn't at all appealing. He'd walk down to the beach, he decided. The ocean always calmed him.

A feeling of foreboding followed Ben like a dark shadow as he hurried out of the office. Aldo Cardano was protective of his daughters, understandably. How much of what Gemma said would he believe?

Ben very much wanted to call Sera and tell her what had occurred, but he decided it was wiser to wait until he spoke to Aldo again. That way, the thing would have some resolution.

But as he strode along the boardwalk beside the water, the sense of impending danger increased.

GEMMA HAD fallen asleep on the drive home, drugged by the sedative Ben had injected. She vaguely remembered her father carrying her into the house, her mother settling her on the couch in the living room.

She awoke now to the muted sound of their voices in the kitchen.

"Halsey wouldn't say what had happened, and Gemma couldn't tell me...."

"...Sera called yesterday. She told me she was with him last weekend, asked me not to say anything...."

Instantly, Gemma remembered what had happened, the terrible sense of betrayal she'd felt when Ben told her it was Sera he cared about. He'd even gone to San Diego to see her, while all the time he'd been sending the poetry here, to Gemma. He'd been deceiving both of them.

Papa had to be told. Papa would know what to do.

The pain of betrayal and the fury she'd felt came back full force, and she struggled up. She steadied herself on a table and then on the hallway door-jamb, as she headed for her bedroom and the box containing the poetry.

Although she was dizzy and disoriented, she made it back to the kitchen, where she flopped down in a chair, put the box with the poems in front of Maria and pulled off the lid.

Tears started again, tears of frustration and anger. She gestured to her mother for a pen and paper.

She had to show her parents how dishonest Ben had been.

Her mother read first one poem, then the next, her brow furrowed.

"Where did these come from, Gemma?"

Halsey, Gemma wrote with violent strokes. *He wrote these, sent them to me....*

Maria studied Gemma's face for a long moment. Then she handed the sheets of paper to Aldo, and he read them, his mouth tight, slapping each down on the table as he finished it.

Gemma wrote, *You see why I thought...and he said things, too, that made me believe...*

"How do you know it was the doctor, Gemma?" Maria's tone was neutral.

Gemma glared at her mother. Why didn't Maria ever just believe her? Why did she always have to question everything? Papa never did; he took her word for it.

I don't know anybody else who'd write this stuff, she scrawled. They started coming right after the accident, and he's been making out with Sera, too. He's been lying to both of us...he's one of these weirdos who want to make it with twins. Sera and I've met some before.

Aldo's face went grim. His jaw tensed as he read Gemma's words. "He can't get away with this. He's a doctor." Aldo's tone and the expression on his face made it clear how furious he was. "Ryngard—he's on the hospital board. He was the one I dealt with when they hired Cardano's for the construction.''

"Aldo, wait. Don't do anything too fast." Maria's face was troubled. "What if someone else wrote these. What if—" she picked up a poem and held it out to her husband "—what if maybe, say, it was Jack?"

Gemma threw herself back in her chair and rolled her eyes. That was *so* ridiculous. Jack was a machine operator; he had no education. There was no way he could write poetry like this.

"Kilgallin?" Aldo's face mirrored Gemma's feelings. "No, Maria. That's crazy talk. Jack's on my crew. He'd never write…" He pointed at the poems and swore in Italian.

It was a relief for Gemma to hear that her father thought exactly the same way she did.

"Jack's a good man," Aldo went on. "A good, hard worker, but all this romance stuff?" Contemptuously he waved a hand again at the poetry. "Jack's no sweet-talking phony. Gemma's right. This comes from that goddamned Halsey. He thinks he can make a fool of my girls." He shoved his chair back and got to his feet, sending it crashing to the floor. He cursed, a long stream of Italian. "He's not getting away with this."

Maria tried to stop him, but Aldo stormed out.

Gemma's head was aching. She needed to go

back to bed and sleep off the medication. She stood up, but her mother caught her hand and held it, staring up into Gemma's eyes.

"*Cara,* I know you've been through a lot, but this is serious, what you're saying about the doctor. Did he kiss you or touch you? Did he do anything to make you think he cared? Besides these." She gestured at the poetry. "Because your sister really likes this man. I know from her voice on the telephone."

Sera. For Mama, it was always about Sera.

The wound was an old one, and it tore open as Gemma jerked her hand away. Hysterically, she nodded over and over, yes, yes, yes, Ben had led her to believe he cared.

He held me in his arms, she wrote. It was the truth; he had held her today. She remembered the strength of those arms, restraining her. As she hurried to her bedroom, sobs tearing through her body, she was unable to admit even to herself how wrong her assumptions had been.

SERA TRIED to subdue the irritation she felt. "Pasquale's decided the scene in the living room will take place in the kitchen, instead," she told her crew. Her boss's sudden changes of venue were making her nuts. She'd just get all the details of a scene mapped out and he'd change his mind about where it should be shot.

"Now we need to locate a wood-burning kitchen stove, kettles, pots, maybe one of those irons they used to heat up on the stove, and a wooden table—for starters. Damn, there goes my cell."

Impatiently, she pulled it out of her handbag.

"Hi, Mama." Apprehension rippled through her. Maria never called her on her cell, always overly conscious that it would cost Sera money.

"Mama, what's wrong?"

Sera listened, frowned, shook her head at the barrage of words. "Mama, please, slow down and start from the beginning. Gemma says *what?*"

She moved away from the crew, turning her back for privacy. As she listened again, her fingers tightened on the phone. Shock rippled through her.

"Let's see if I got this right, Mama. Gemma's been getting love poems, and she thinks Ben wrote them? What makes her think that? Did you read them? Did *you* talk to Gemma about this, Mama?" Aldo always took Gemma's word for things, but Mama didn't. Maria looked deeper, questioned more.

Beginning to feel sick, Sera heard her mother explain that whoever had written the poems was definitely pretending to be in love with Gemma.

At Sera's insistence, Maria read several of them over the phone.

Sera tried to imagine Ben writing them. She didn't know if he wrote poetry; it wasn't something she'd thought to ask. Would these be the sort he'd write? They weren't great, but they weren't the work of a rank amateur, either.

With a knot in her stomach, she remembered that he'd had volumes of poetry in his condo, on the makeshift shelves beside his bed. Every muscle in her body tensed when her mother told her that Gemma truly believed Ben had come on to her. Of course, Maria didn't phrase it that way; she said that the doctor had "made a pass" at Gemma, taken her in his arms. Whatever the language, the meaning was the same.

Maria went on to say that Aldo was in a rage, that he'd gone to one of the hospital administrators to complain about Ben's actions.

Sera was stunned at how quickly everything was falling apart. She burst out, "But shouldn't Papa have talked to Ben first?"

Sera couldn't help but think of the ugly ramifications of this whole mess for Ben. Part of her just couldn't believe that he'd done what Gemma was accusing him of. But in the back of her mind was the memory of how visibly relieved he'd been when she'd insisted she was a career woman, not interested in a long-term relationship.

Some demon had kept wondering if that meant he was dating other women as well as her. She'd never dared to ask; he'd seemed so honest with her, so—infatuated.

He's a love-'em-and-leave-'em sort of guy. The word is he deals in multiples, one after the other after the other.

If he'd dated that many women, maybe twins represented a whole new challenge for Ben?

Sera shuddered. *Was* he the type of man who considered the sexual conquest of twins a major notch on his belt? She didn't think so, but how could she be sure? Vancouver and San Diego were a long ways apart, and she really hadn't known him very long.

Her mother was asking her to come home, saying that Sera needed to talk to Gemma herself, to get to the bottom of this. Sera forced herself to think about the set, and whether or not she could take the weekend off.

"I'll try, Mama. I'll phone and let you know." Sick to her very soul, she hung up.

"I could start calling stores," the young gofer suggested.

Sera looked at her, totally unable to figure out what the girl was talking about. She felt icy-cold and shaky, as shocked as if she'd been in a smashup.

Maybe she had.

If Ben had done what Gemma insisted, then Sera had just suffered a serious collision of the heart.

THE PHONE CALL from Earl Ryngard came just as Ben was preparing to leave the office.

Ryngard was the chief of staff who headed up the Medical Advisory Committee at St. Joe's. That he had rigorous standards for both dignity and morality among physicians was well-known, and he'd made it apparent that he disapproved greatly of Ben's and Greg's high-spirited antics before Greg's accident and subsequent marriage to Lily.

He'd never come out and said openly that he considered their behavior a disgrace to the hospital, but his attitude was clear. He was always formally polite to Ben, but Ben sensed an undercurrent of disdain and censure.

Ben had often seen Ryngard having lunch with Roderick Miller, Vera's uncle, and Ben was certain Miller had given Ryngard his version of Ben's marriage to, mistreatment of and divorce from his niece.

The very fact that he was calling put Ben on guard.

They exchanged pleasantries, but a certain note of triumph in the other man's voice alarmed Ben, and he got to the point quickly. "What can I do for you, Earl?"

"There's been a complaint, Ben, and I wanted to speak to you about it before mentioning it to anyone else."

Ben's heart sank. He thought he knew what it involved; he'd tried repeatedly to speak to Aldo Cardano, with no success. The other man had turned his cell phone off and only the answering machine responded at his home number. Ben had planned to visit the construction site in the hope of seeing Cardano.

"It seems a female patient has suggested there may have been sexual misconduct during your treatment of her." Ryngard could barely conceal his satisfaction. "Her father is a man I know and respect, and he came to me directly." Ryngard's voice had taken on an unctuous quality that set Ben's teeth on edge. "Of course the board is under obligation to take any such suggestion very seriously indeed. As a fellow physician, I felt it only fair to ask you for your side of the story."

"We're discussing Ms. Gemma Cardano—is that correct?"

Ryngard confirmed that it was.

Although Ben's heart was hammering, he forced his voice to sound totally neutral as he summarized and repeated exactly what had happened between Gemma and him.

"I assure you there was absolutely nothing inappropriate in my dealings with Ms. Cardano," Ben concluded.

"Her father mentioned the existence of, humph, certain poetry of a romantic nature," Ryngard said. "He says his daughter is convinced you wrote it."

"Well, his daughter is wrong." Ben's control was slipping. "I don't know anything about this poetry, and I can assure you that writing poetry and mailing it to my female patients is not one of my pastimes.''

"Yes. Well, of course we're left with the nasty reality that this is your word against hers, Ben. Perhaps it would help if you spoke to Mr. Cardano directly. The board prefers that complaints of this nature be handled immediately if possible. They can be most damaging to the hospital's reputation.''

Ben held on to his temper with the utmost difficulty.

"I've been trying to do exactly that all day, with no success. Mr. Cardano has evidently decided not to speak to me,'' he replied between clenched teeth.

"Yes. Well. That's most unfortunate, because Mr. Cardano said that he's also considering going to the newspapers. And making a complaint to the College of Physicians and Surgeons.''

Ben could hardly believe what he was hearing. "In other words, he wants me tarred and feathered and run out of town.''

Ryngard'd laugh was gloating. "He did say he doesn't think you should be practicing. I don't want to sound precipitate here, Ben, but it might be a good idea to contact a lawyer, just to clarify exactly where you stand on this matter.'' Obviously Ryngard was thoroughly enjoying this.

Ben ignored his suggestion. "To my knowledge, a complaint of this nature has to be more than in-

sinuation and innuendo. *What Ms. Cardano's say-*
ing about me is simply not true.'' Ben's voice had
risen, and the knuckles on the hand gripping the
receiver were white. "She has absolutely not a
shred of evidence to back up her accusations."

"Of course, of course. Seeing a lawyer was just
a suggestion." Ryngard mouthed a few more pat-
ently insincere platitudes and assurances and finally
hung up.

Ben was trembling. With extreme care, he set the
phone down and it rang again almost instantly.

Ben snatched it up, thinking it might be Aldo
Cardano, but Greg's voice greeted him, instead.

"Lily's feeling a bit under the weather today so
I'm gonna make dinner. You wanna come over and
keep her and Stanley company while I cook? We're
keen to hear all about the San Diego connection."

During the conversation with Ryngard, Ben had
made up his mind to go straight to the Cardanos'
house and do his best to straighten out the entire
mess. Now he hesitated. Maybe talking this whole
thing out with friends first was a good idea.

"I'd like to come, but I have to feed Grendel and
make a phone call." Whatever else happened, he
had to speak to Sera, and right away.

"Anytime. We're having a swim before dinner.
We'll probably be down by the pool."

Ben thanked Greg and hung up, took a deep
breath and then dialed Sera's cell number.

"Hello?" Her husky voice brought such a powerful visual image of having her in his arms that for a moment he couldn't respond. He closed his eyes and tried to figure out what to say to her, how to make her believe him.

"Hello?" Her voice was now impatient.

"Sera, it's me."

"Oh, Ben. Hello." Her voice was cool and distant, and he knew instantly that someone had already spoken to her. Worse yet, he suspected Sera believed what she'd heard.

A sense of utter desperation came over him, and suddenly the only thing that mattered was convincing her he was innocent of the ridiculous accusations her sister was making.

CHAPTER SIXTEEN

"SERA, there's been a terrible misunderstanding here, and I wanted to talk to you about it." Ben wished with all his heart that he didn't have to do this by telephone.

"My mother called. She told me what happened." There was an accusatory note in Sera's voice. "She said Gemma was so upset she had to be sedated."

"That's true." A desperate urgency came over Ben. That she listen, that she believe him, was enormously important. "But what Gemma's saying is just not so, Sera. I did nothing whatsoever to make her believe I was attracted to her."

"She says you made a pass at her, that you held her in your arms, that you wrote her poetry." Sera's voice trembled.

Ben's hands clenched, and he tried to suppress the righteous anger he felt. He didn't want to come right out and insist to Sera that her sister was lying. It would only make her defensive. And as Ryngard had gleefully pointed out, it really came down to Gemma's word against his.

"Sera, I didn't do a single thing that could have been misunderstood. Certainly I held Gemma in my arms to restrain her—she'd become violent in my office. As for the poetry, I honestly don't know what she's talking about.''

A long silence. Ben waited, his emotions in a turmoil. To have to defend himself in this fashion infuriated him. He wanted to roar at Sera that innocence was usually presumed until guilt was proven. He wanted to beg her to give him a chance.

She was silent.

"I've tried all day to contact your father,'' he finally said as quietly as he could manage. "I'd like to explain myself to him, but I haven't been able to reach him.'' He didn't add that Aldo had already made a complaint to Ryngard; that wasn't Sera's affair. It was an issue Ben planned to take up with Cardano. The other man should at least have given him the opportunity to defend himself before he'd gone to Ryngard, and Ben planned to tell him as much.

Right now, however, the thing Ben most wanted was to somehow convince Sera he was telling the truth. He didn't understand why that was imperative, why it meant so much to him that this woman believe him, that she trust him.

"Goddamn it,'' he burst out when the silence lengthened again. "I despise telephones at a time like this.'' He needed to be with her, to see the expression on her face, watch her luminous eyes; Sera had eyes that reflected her every emotion. He remembered making love with her, looking down into those eyes, meeting her somewhere beyond sensation.

If only he had a chance to hold her right now, he had the feeling everything would be all right. She'd know he was telling the truth if she was face-to-face with him. "You *do* believe me, Sera?"

He heard her sigh.

"I think so." But she sounded tentative. "I'm just not sure, Ben. It's really hard to know what to believe when I'm this far away. I'm flying home Saturday afternoon. Maybe we could talk when I'm in Vancouver."

To know that at least she wanted to talk, that she was coming to Vancouver, that he'd see her in just a couple days time, was a huge relief. His spirits lifted a little. "Tell me what flight you're on. I'll meet you at the airport."

"Thanks, but I can't do that, Ben. I'm only coming because my mother insisted. She's very upset about all this. My family will be picking me up."

"Okay. I'll phone you. We can arrange to meet. Where will you be staying?" He longed to suggest she stay with him, but he knew it wasn't possible.

"At my parents' house. I have to go, Ben. We're still working. They're calling for me. Bye."

He heard the connection sever, and she was gone before he could say anything further.

"BEN, OLD BUDDY, you need a good lawyer. And you need one right away." Greg turned to Lily. "Who's that woman who was representing Philips on the malpractice charge?"

"Faye Weaver." Lily watched placidly as Greg patiently sponged up the glass of milk Stanley had just dumped all over the table.

"It was an assident, Mommy. I didn't mean to spill." Stanley gave his mother a repentant look from under his long lashes. "I 'pologize."

"I know, sweetheart. It's okay. Daddy will get you more."

Greg righted the glass and Ben absently filled it with milk. "It's too late to get hold of her at her office. I'm gonna call Philips and see if he's got her home number." Greg dialed and a few moments later handed Ben both the portable phone and a scribbled number.

Ben took it reluctantly. He didn't want this thing to escalate, he didn't want to make it bigger than it already was, and he was afraid that hiring a lawyer would do exactly that.

"Call," Greg insisted. "If it turns out to be nothing, fine. But with Ryngard involved already, I'd cover my back. He's Miller's friend, and you know as well as I do that Miller will do whatever he can to sink you.''

Ben hesitated, detesting the idea of having to repeat the entire sordid story to a lawyer. In some warped fashion, it felt disloyal to Sera.

''What do you think, Lily?'' Maybe a woman would see things differently.

She'd been exceptionally quiet during Ben's recital of the facts. In fact, she'd been quiet all afternoon.

''I agree with Greg. Something like this can mushroom. It wouldn't hurt to have a lawyer involved right away. And Faye Weaver's probably familiar with the politics at St. Joe's. Her sister's married to Banfield.'' Conrad Banfield was head of the psychiatric unit.

''Okay, I'll call her.'' He did, and got a machine. He left his cell number and reluctantly added that the matter was urgent.

''What means *urgent,* Uncle Ben?'' Stanley had a milk ring around his mouth. He was wearing only a pair of blue swimming trunks, with a red Superman cape around his neck. It kept getting in the way, which accounted for the food around his chair and the spilled milk. Lily had suggested he take it off, but she hadn't pressed the matter when he refused.

''*Urgent* means you want something right now,'' Ben explained.

"I need to go for ice cream. It's *urgent*." Stanley beamed, delighted with himself.

"Maybe we'll all go for ice cream," Greg suggested. "You up to it, Lil?"

"Why don't you guys go," Lily suggested. "I'd like to lie down for a little while, maybe have a nap."

Greg frowned at his wife. "You feeling okay, sweetheart?"

"Absolutely. Just very pregnant is all." She reached out a hand and patted his arm, smiling at him, and Ben's heart twisted in his chest. What would it be like to have a woman you loved smile that way at you? To have your woman big with the baby you'd made together?

"My cell will be on," Greg assured her. "If you need anything, call."

"You're not exactly going on safari," Lily laughed. "Although maybe you should put on shorts and a shirt with that cape, Super Stanley."

"Is it *urgent?*"

Everyone chorused that yes, it was urgent. Stanley reluctantly struggled into clothing as the men cleared up the dishes and tidied the kitchen.

A short while later Ben and Greg were sitting in an ice-cream parlor watching Stanley devour a bowl of chocolate ice cream when Greg's cell phone buzzed.

He answered it, listened, and his face paled. He

barked out several questions, and Ben could see his hand trembling as he ended the call.

"Lily's water broke. The pains are coming one on top of the other. She's phoned for an ambulance. It's on its way. I'm calling the ER to tell them I'll be there right away."

He did and then Greg scooped up his son and made a dash for the van. Ben thought to grab Stanley's ice cream before he followed them.

"I'll drive," Ben offered. Greg was visibly upset, face pale, jaw set. "I'll drop you at Emerg and then take Stanley home."

"Judith should be home soon. She's at her nightschool class."

"I'll stay with him. I can spend the night if you want."

Greg shook his head. "You've got Grendel. Judith's fine on her own with Stanley." His jaw clenched. "I only hope Lily's okay. I should never have left her alone. I should have guessed something was wrong. The baby's coming too soon. Lil's only thirty-three weeks."

Thirty-seven was considered full-term.

"Who's her OB-GYN?"

"Morgan Gilbert. Lily called her. Morgan's waiting at Emerg. Trust Lil to have everything under control, even when she's the patient."

"Morgan's the best there is."

Greg nodded, but Ben could tell he wasn't really

listening. His friend was undoubtedly imagining all the dreadful complications that Lily and his child might develop.

Ben knew from personal experience that the horrific part of being a doctor when someone you cared about was a patient was knowing exactly how many things could go wrong. He'd driven himself nuts worrying about spinal injury and brain damage when Greg had been hurt in the skiing accident.

"*Please* can I have my ice cream when we get home?" Stanley's voice was plaintive from his car seat in the back of the van. "It's *urgent*."

"You sure can, sport." Greg explained to his son that Mommy had to go to the hospital because the baby was coming, and that, yes, it was urgent that Daddy get there right away.

Ben pulled up beside St. Joe's Emergency entrance and Greg leaped out and ran into the building.

Ben had just pulled back into traffic when his cell phone rang. It was the lawyer, Faye Weaver. He turned into a side street and parked, then outlined exactly what had happened with Gemma Cardano, and also related his conversation with Earl Ryngard. Weaver asked perceptive questions, particularly what action, if any, Ben had taken thus far.

"None. I've been trying to contact Mr. Cardano and tell him what actually happened, but he's obviously decided not to speak to me. My first inclination has been to confront the Cardano family and somehow force Gemma to tell the truth.''

''No.'' Her voice was firm. ''You absolutely must not do that. Mr. Cardano sounds to me as though he could be very confrontational. We don't want this matter to escalate any more than it already has. Let me contact Mr. Cardano for you and find out exactly what it is he's after.''

That wasn't hard to figure out, Ben thought bitterly. Cardano was after his hide. He wanted him to give up practicing medicine.

''Uncle Ben, I have to pee. It's *urgent.*''

''Okay, Stanley. Look, Ms. Weaver, I'm gonna have to go.''

''Do you or do you not wish for me to represent you in this matter?''

''Uncle Ben, I really *really* urgent need to pee.''

''Yes, Stanley, we're going home right now. Hold on, okay, sport?'' What should he do? What decision should he make about this incredible debacle?

''Yes, Ms. Weaver, I do. I do want you to represent me.'' With a sinking sensation in his gut, Ben disconnected the call and started the van.

IT WAS PAST NINE that evening by the time Judith got home. Ben, with immense gratitude and relief, turned over Stanley's care to her.

He was exhausted; his godson had just gone to sleep ten minutes before. Stanley had thrown a major tantrum when he found out his ice cream had melted into a puddle on the long drive to the house. He'd also wet himself in the van, and it took some doing for Ben to convince the little boy that a bath was in order and it was time for pajamas.

"I want my mommy," he'd insisted, bottom lip trembling. "I want my daddy. I want my ice cream."

Ben could supply only one of those items. In desperation, he called a cab company and had the driver pick up a tub of chocolate ice-cream, packed in ice, and deliver it. When it arrived, Ben mounded some onto a cone, a box of which he found in a kitchen cupboard, and Stanley was mollified. He ate it slowly, eyes almost closing between mouthfuls.

Ben tucked him into bed, read a favorite book about monsters twice through, and at last, thumb firmly plugged, the little boy slept. Ben wished he could crawl in beside him, close his eyes and erase the day.

After leaving the Brulottes' house, Ben drove straight to St. Joe's and made his way up to the maternity floor. He arrived just in time to congratulate Greg and Lily on the safe arrival of their tiny daughter.

"She's perfect. Look at her." Greg beamed. "Lungs are great. She did eight on the Apgar. Morgan says she's like a full-term baby. And Lily's fine. She went through it all like a trooper. We're calling the baby Hannah, after Lily's grandma. Here, take her.''

Greg plunked the blanket-wrapped baby into Ben's arms. The tiny girl's blue eyes were wide-open, and she was gazing around at the world. She had a full head of straight, dark hair, and she seemed to give Ben a quizzical look.

''Hello, little Hannah. Welcome to the world.'' Ben grinned down at the baby, and for a magical moment the problems and concerns of the day disappeared in the miracle of birth.

On the drive home through the warm summer night, he thought of the baby Hannah, and Sera's face appeared in his mind's eye. Witnessing Greg and Lily's happiness with each other and with their new daughter had made Ben lonely in a way he'd never been before. He thought about Sera coming to Vancouver, and how very much he wanted to see her.

And then, for some unknown reason, he thought of Vera and the baby they'd lost so many years before. Tears filled his eyes and overflowed, and he mopped at them with his wrist, embarrassed by this rush of powerful emotion.

Why did that memory come back to haunt him now? How could that ill-fated marriage still be causing him problems? But it was—in the form of

Ryngard and his association with Vera's uncle, Roderick Miller.

Ben realized that he'd never really apologized to Vera. He'd given her all the material possessions they'd amassed together; he'd willingly paid her alimony for five years; but he'd never said in so many words that he was sorry for what had happened to her.

He steered his truck across the Cambie Street Bridge. An apology wouldn't make any difference to anything. What had happened was in the past. They were both different people by now; to dredge it all up again wasn't logical.

But by the time he pulled into his parking slot of his apartment in Gastown he knew that, logical or not, apologizing to his ex-wife was something that he simply had to do. In some obscure fashion, making peace with Vera had everything to do with his feelings about Sera. He wasn't clear how or why; he knew only it was necessary.

And if he was going to do it, he'd better get at it right away, before he lost his courage.

CHAPTER SEVENTEEN

BEN WORKED the following day, grateful for a demanding surgery that absorbed all his time and attention in the morning. In the afternoon he had back-to-back patient appointments that left no opportunity to worry, or even to make personal phone calls. He was aware that he hadn't yet telephoned Sera and made a firm arrangement to see her when she was in Vancouver. He was putting it off, half afraid that she'd reconsidered and decided not to see him after all.

After work he drove home, fed Grendel and immediately dialed her number. Her cell phone wasn't turned on, so he called the motel and left a message for her to phone him as soon as she got home.

He waited all evening, postponing Grendel's walk. He called her twice more before eleven but was unable to make contact. It was almost one and he'd just gone to bed when the phone finally rang.

"Ben?" She was apologetic. "Forgive me for phoning so late. I just got in. We were shooting on location in a little town in the desert and the battery on my cell phone died. There was a note on my door, asking me to call you.''

"I'm glad you did.'' He propped pillows behind his head, and Grendel, on the bed beside him, rumbled his annoyance. "How are you, Sera?''

"I'm okay.'' But her voice was brittle. "Listen, Ben, I've been thinking. It's probably best all round if I don't see you this weekend.''

His body tensed. "Why's that?''

She didn't answer directly. "Did you know my dad's already complained to someone at St. Joe's?''

"Yeah, the guy talked to me. But that doesn't have anything to do with you seeing me.'' Was this panic roiling in his gut?

"It does, though.'' He detected embarrassment in her tone. "I told Papa I thought he was wrong to do what he did. I told him I believed you, but no matter what I personally think, they're still my family. If I go on seeing you, I'll be caught in the middle of all this, and I don't want to be.''

He heard her take in a quavering breath, but her voice was firm when she added, "Pasquale's offered me a permanent job with his company. I'll be based in L.A., and won't be coming to Vancouver much. And it's not as if there's anything serious between us, Ben. We both agreed that our careers came first. You said in the beginning you weren't interested in long-term.''

He *had* said that, goddamn it. He always said that.

"What can I say to make you change your mind?"

"Nothing, Ben. I just think it's time we ended it."

He swung his legs to the floor, gripping the phone as if it were an enemy to be vanquished, and drew in a breath to argue with her. Then it dawned on him with a shock of recognition that she was using *his* tactics against him.

He'd done this countless times himself—reached the point where a relationship had to end, phoned and tried his best to be gracious and firm at the same time, struggled through the awkwardness and pain and prayed for the call to end quickly.

His pride came to his rescue. "If that's your decision, I guess there's nothing for me to do but accept it." The words were like gall in his mouth.

"Thanks." A heartbeat later she said softly, "Bye, Ben." There might have been a sob in her voice, but maybe he was only imagining what he wanted to hear. The connection ended.

He swore, a long stream of profanity, and drove his fist into the mattress. Grendel yelped in protest and slunk off the bed.

Ben couldn't lie down again. He couldn't stay in the loft, either. He dragged on shorts and a shirt.

"C'mon, boy. We're going walking."

Grendel bounded off the bed and found his leash, wagging his tail so hard his entire body shook.

As Ben strode through the nearly deserted streets, he tried to tell himself that this was for the best. Eventually, he would have told Sera it was over. Better that it should end now, before they got into it any deeper, he reasoned.

His brain went on and on with logic, but with every step his heart seemed to grow heavier in his chest. Images of Sera flashed like silent movies through his mind. Grendel finally grew tired and started to lag, but Ben increased his pace, trying unsuccessfully to leave the pain and sense of loss behind.

The thing that became more and more clear with every step was his conviction that in order to go ahead he would have to go back. He just had to make his peace with Vera.

Friday morning, he had Dana cancel his afternoon appointments. As soon as his surgery was done, he drove to North Vancouver. He'd made inquiries; now it wasn't difficult to find the bakery where Vera worked. He pulled up in a spot across the street and parked. Instead of getting out immediately, he sat there, staring across at the striped awning, heart hammering as cravenly he hoped that maybe she wouldn't be at work today.

Coming here had been hard. It was about the last

thing he'd wanted to do, but something had driven him.

At last he made his way across the street and into the small shop.

Two customers were buying bread and sausage rolls, and for an instant Ben didn't realize the woman serving them was Vera. It wasn't until she smiled at them and assured them the sausage rolls had been made that morning that Ben recognized her voice.

When they were married she'd been petite, bone slender, with long silvery-blond straight hair that he'd loved to touch. Now she was heavy, and her hair had turned shiny white. It was short and tightly permed. Her face was still pretty, but the extra weight made her look older than she was. She wore a voluminous white apron over a cheerful yellow dress.

The customers left, and she turned to him with a professional smile that faded into shock when she recognized him.

"Hello, Vera." He moved closer to the counter.

"Ben?" Her face paled. She put her plump hands on the counter, as if to support herself. "Ben. What—what are you doing here?"

"I came to see you." Would she order him out? Would she become hysterical? He hadn't planned what to say, hadn't gone further than just making this journey.

His throat was dry. "I hoped we could talk, Vera."

She stared at him for what seemed an eternity, her silvery-gray eyes hard to read. At last she nodded.

"Okay. I'll get Lisa to watch the counter for me." She disappeared through the door to the back. A young girl in jeans and a white T-shirt came out and began to cheerfully serve an old man and a young girl who'd walked in while Ben waited.

It felt like a long time before Vera reappeared. Her apron was gone and she'd obviously brushed her hair and applied fresh lipstick. A pair of red sunglasses perched in her curly hair. She led the way out the door to the street.

"There's a park at the end of the block. We can go there," she suggested.

"Good." Ben followed her along the sidewalk, desperately groping for something to say and coming up empty. "It's a great day," he finally blurted.

"We're having good luck with the weather this summer," she agreed. After that they walked along in silence.

The park overlooked the inlet. The sun glinted off the water, and Vera sat down on a wooden bench and tipped the glasses down onto her nose.

"Why the visit now, Ben? After all this time?"

Here it was; here was his opportunity. The words

were easy, as if he'd been unconsciously rehearsing them for a long while.

"I want to apologize to you, Vera. I want to tell you I'm truly sorry for the things that happened between us." It was a huge relief to say it. "I wasn't much of a husband to you."

She smiled a little and shook her head. "Nope, you sure weren't."

Her simple words confirmed what he already knew, yet he was surprised that she didn't sound angry. Instead, she seemed resigned. He wished she'd take off her glasses so he could see the expression in her eyes. He had more to say to her, and it would be difficult. He took a breath and let it out.

"I'm sorry about the baby, too. I should have been more understanding. I should have valued it more—valued *you* more." He struggled on. "I was ambitious. All I could think of was going to India, getting the training and experience I needed, getting on with my career. It was egotistical and selfish of me."

"I certainly thought so at the time." She turned her head away and gazed out at the ocean, her thoughts impossible to read. "I was about as unhappy as a person could get. But I didn't realize at that stage that I had a form of mental illness. All I could do was be mad at you and sorry for myself." There was acceptance in her tone, and forgiveness for the troubled girl she'd been. "The miscarriage and then the divorce pushed me over a narrow ledge I'd been walking for years. That was my first real break. I've had two more since then. That first one was the worst, though, because I didn't know what to expect."

She sounded almost placid. Ben waited for the anger he knew she must feel, the anger he knew he deserved.

"I hated you for a long time, Ben. I blamed you for everything, but I finally found a good doctor who wouldn't give up on me. With his help I admitted that I had an illness, and then I began taking responsibility for my actions." She turned and gave him a wry grin. "That didn't happen for years, though. My mom and dad didn't make it easy for me. They never admitted there was anything wrong with me. They always believed my mental illness was something *you* did to me. It was easier just to blame you for everything, and for a long time I bought into that."

"And now?" Talking with her was getting easier. He was even beginning to relax a bit. Her openness, her honesty, pleasantly surprised him.

"Oh, now I see that what happened at that time was inevitable. I'm still sorry about our baby, but what kind of mother could I have been? Lordie, it's taken me years just to get on a drug regimen that works for me. When I think of trying to raise a kid in the midst of that, I really know that things happen for the best.''

"But you never went back to nursing. I've always felt bad about that. You were such a great nurse.''

She shrugged. ''It was my own choice. I always knew I didn't do well with shift work. Stress and lack of sleep really affect my condition, so I decided to work at the bakery.'' There was quiet pride in her voice when she added, ''It's mine now, you know. Natalie and her husband moved to Seattle and I bought them out. I'm planning to turn it into a coffee shop.'' She was clearly excited about it. ''I've leased the space next door. I'll knock the wall down and put in tables and serve soup and sandwiches.''

''That's a great idea.'' He was trying to match this quiet, determined woman to the image he'd had in his mind of his disturbed and resentful child-wife. It wasn't easy. All his preconceived notions, all the negative things he'd heard via the hospital grapevine, were proving false.

''You never remarried, Vera.''

''Nope. But that doesn't mean I don't have someone in my life.'' She smiled at him. ''Dean's a lawyer. We've been a couple for four years now. Neither of us sees marriage as something we want to do just yet, but eventually we will. And not marrying has nothing to do with what happened between *us,* if that's what you're thinking." She gave him a curious glance.

"How about you, Ben? I don't keep up with the people I used to know at the hospital anymore. Last I heard you were a carefree bachelor with a beachfront house that was the site of great parties."

He grimaced and shook his head. "The parties are over, although I'm still single." He explained about moving into a Gastown condo. "I've got a dog," he added, thinking to himself how pathetic that sounded, as if he'd turned into the sort of man who poured all his affections out only on an animal.

They chatted for another half hour, and then Vera looked at her watch and got to her feet.

"I have to get back. Lisa's good, but she hasn't been working for me long enough to take over completely." She held out a hand, and Ben held it clasped in his for a long moment.

"I'm glad you came, Ben. You threw me for a loop at first, but it's past time we talked."

There was one last thing he needed to ask.

"Your uncle who's on the hospital board, Dr. Miller. He's always made it pretty clear that he blames me for ruining your life." He hesitated, wanting to ask if she felt that way, too. She answered before he could go on.

"You probably know Uncle Rod hates you with a passion," she said matter-of-factly. "He needs to blame somebody for what happened to me, and I guess you're available. I've tried to talk to him about it, but he won't listen. You probably don't remember my telling you, but he sort of adopted me after he and his wife lost their only daughter. He was really proud when I graduated from nursing school. After Cindy died he became a workaholic. Eventually Auntie Hilda left him for another man. Uncle Rod never got over it. He moved out here from Toronto about the time we broke up, and when I had my breakdown, it was one more thing to add to his injustice list. It's always easier to blame somebody else than to accept responsibility yourself.'' She smiled at him. ''I should know. I did it myself for a pile of years.''

''But not now.'' It was almost impossible to believe.

''Nope.'' She shook her head. ''Time comes when you have to grow up. It took me a while, but I finally got on with my life.'' She touched his arm. ''Bye, Ben. This has been good for both of us. I'm glad you came.''

He watched her ample figure hurry off down the street, and he sat back down on the bench, shocked at the discrepancy between what he'd thought to be true and what actually was.

He'd always envisioned Vera as the troubled young bride he'd married and deserted, and the memory had never failed to bring up pangs of guilt and self-loathing.

The truth was, Vera had gone on with her life, in spite of an illness that was difficult and unpredictable. She'd grown into a mature and honest woman, with a job she obviously enjoyed and a life that included someone she loved. He didn't need to feel guilty about her. He hadn't wrecked her life, as he'd always felt he had.

How arrogant of him to think he had that power over her. His face burned, and he knew it wasn't from the sun; he was embarrassed at how stupid and self-centered he'd been.

And if he was being honest, he also had to face the fact that Vera had formed a long-lasting relationship with someone she clearly loved, while he'd used their failed marriage as an excuse to build a wall between himself and anything that looked the least bit like commitment.

He'd stubbornly kept it in place, even though it had started to wobble when he met Sera.

The desolate emptiness that had plagued him ever since her phone call came back now, intensified because of what he'd learned about himself this afternoon.

The question was, what was he going to do with that knowledge? Could he win Sera back? He began plotting ways and means, but what troubled him the most was that part of what she'd said was irrefutable.

Sera was committed to her career, and so was he.

Her work would now keep her in California, while his was based in Vancouver. The other issues, the ones with Gemma and Aldo Cardano, could somehow be resolved, but figuring out a solution to the geographical problem seemed impossible. He mulled his predicament over, sitting slumped on the bench in the sunshine, and all of a sudden he realized what he was doing.

For the first time since his marriage to Vera, he was thinking commitment. He was plotting ways in which he and Sera could be together, not for just a month or two, not even for a year.

He was thinking *always,* and the realization both stunned and thrilled him.

CHAPTER EIGHTEEN

BY SATURDAY EVENING, Sera heartily wished she'd stayed in California instead of coming home. Her family was making her crazy.

Her father was at his very worst, bombastic and unwilling to listen to anything except his own version of what had gone on between Gemma and Ben. Each time he retold the story of finding Gemma sedated and hysterical in Ben's office, he became more agitated. He tried to pry out of Sera the details of her relationship with Ben, and when she wouldn't tell him, he hollered at her about loyalty and family pride and responsibility to her sister.

Maria was obviously angry with Aldo, slamming dishes on the table, clucking in disapproval at his ranting, but she didn't come out and really say exactly what she felt or believed.

Gemma, on the other hand, seemed uncharacteristically subdued. Sera had been certain that as soon as she saw her sister, she'd know beyond a doubt whether Gemma was lying about Ben. And she had known; Sera was now convinced that Gemma believed what she'd said about the poetry.

How could that be? There was no way her sister could deceive her; Sera could tell when Gemma was lying, and right now she wasn't.

As soon as they got home from the airport, Gemma had dumped out the poems on the bed in their old bedroom. Sera had read them, dreading this moment, terrified that she'd find some word or phrase that would prove to her Ben had written them.

They were touching in their simple message of unrequited love, but she detected absolutely nothing of the Ben she knew in them. Sera told first Gemma and then her parents that she was sure Ben hadn't written them, which brought on tears from Gemma and yet another tirade from Aldo. How could Sera be loyal to and protect someone who'd hurt her own sister?

Sera was exhausted, confused and horribly unhappy. The same frantic sense of loss she'd experienced ever since she'd broken off with Ben two days before made her chest ache and her stomach nauseous.

She knew in her heart that cutting off the relationship was the only thing she could have done. Because aside from what Gemma thought had happened, aside from her father's outrage, something else troubled her: the knowledge that whatever she and Ben had shared together hadn't meant any more to him than any other of his casual affairs—and it had to her. She'd fallen in love with Ben Halsey, in spite of her resolutions not to. And regardless of his attentiveness, his eagerness to see her, his obvious desire to be with her, the time would come, sooner or maybe later, but inevitably, when he'd want to move on to his next conquest. And where would that leave her?

So the solution had been clear: get out before she got in any deeper. She'd called him Thursday and said the things that had to be said, and it had ripped her apart. She'd hung up the phone and wrapped her arms around herself, because the sobs she couldn't control felt as though they were ripping her apart. She'd cried most of the night. The next morning the makeup man on the set had kindly done what he could to disguise her swollen eyes and puffy face, and somehow she'd gotten through the day's work.

Since then, the pain had subsided to a dull ache, but being in Vancouver was agony. Knowing Ben was only a fifteen-minute drive away was a temptation she could hardly resist, and when the telephone rang at dinnertime some sixth sense warned her it was him.

Her mother went into the kitchen to answer the call, and without a word beckoned to Sera. Maria obviously realized who it was, but she came back into the dining room and sat down without a word.

As Sera picked up the phone in the kitchen, she

heard Maria begin a loud, long, involved story about a cousin who'd had twins, and she could tell her mother was covering for her, monopolizing the family's attention so Sera could talk without being overheard.

"Sera? It's me, please don't hang up." His familiar voice stabbed at her heart. She turned away from the doorway so her family couldn't see her face, and she listened.

"Sera, I really want to see you. Please say that you'll meet me, speak to me."

She said no, that wasn't possible; no, she couldn't see him; no, she wouldn't change her mind.

"Please don't call here again," she told him with as much dignity as she could muster. Then she said goodbye and knew she was going to be sick. She escaped to the bathroom, where she ran the water hard as dry sobs racked her.

The dreadful evening dragged on and on. Her uncle Victor arrived. He'd heard that Aldo had been called away from the construction site to rescue Gemma, that someone had had to drive her car home, and he wanted to know what it was all about. From the horse's mouth, he demanded.

Aldo launched into the story once more. There had never been any secrets among the Cardano relatives, and Sera knew that when the family gathered tomorrow after church at her aunt Teresa's, the whole thing would be brought up and discussed and argued about all over again, and she didn't think she could bear it.

"I'm going to bed." Hastily, she wished everyone a good-night, and tried to stop herself from racing up the stairs.

A touch on her back made her aware that Gemma was right behind her. They were sharing their old bedroom, sleeping side by side in the twin beds they'd had while they were growing up. Wanting desperately to be alone tonight, Sera felt trapped.

Gemma indicated to Sera that she should use the bathroom first, and when Gemma came out a short while later, Sera was curled up under the bedclothes with her lamp off and her face turned away, pretending sleep.

Sadness had given way to a furious anger at her sister. She'd had it up to her eyeballs with Gemma and her mischief, Sera fumed.

Whether Gemma had intended to cause so much trouble this time, Sera didn't know. Whatever her intentions, though, the results were horrifically painful.

But Gemma came and sat on Sera's bed and switched her light back on, pad and pen in hand. She touched Sera's shoulder, insisting she look at her message.

You really don't think Ben wrote the poetry?

Unwillingly, Sera sat up. She shook her head,

and her tone was harsh. "I told you before, no, I don't think so, Gemma. It doesn't sound like him at all." The last thing she wanted Gemma to know was that she was in love with Ben. Her sister wasn't to be trusted with such a confidence.

Gemma's eyes, so much like her own, studied Sera's face for a long moment. Then she wrote, *He made love to you?*

What was the use? This thing had a life of its own and avoiding it wasn't working.

"Yeah." Sera sighed and nodded. "He did. We had sort of a one-night stand in San Diego. Two nights, actually. Nothing serious," she said, trying to act flippant and failing. She watched the vivid play of emotions on her sister's face, first jealousy, then confusion and, finally, uncertainty.

Sera couldn't stop herself. The anger she felt toward Gemma had reached a point where Sera couldn't contain it any longer. "But he didn't make love with you, Gemma, did he? He didn't try anything with you. What you told Papa wasn't true, was it?" She was shrieking, and she didn't care. "You based the whole stupid drama on those poems. You lied to Papa." Her tone was accusing, and her hands were trembling. She slid them under the duvet and drew her knees up to her chest, knowing it was hopeless to confront her sister. Gemma would deny it all, just as she'd always denied any wrongdoing.

Gemma hesitated for a long time, and then at last, with great reluctance, she nodded.

Sera was astounded. It was the first time she'd ever known her sister to own up.

"Why, Em? Why would you cause so much trouble for a man who never did anything but good for you?"

In spite of herself, Sera's voice rose again. "Look at you. Your face is just exactly the way it was before. That's all because of Ben, his skill, his dedication. You oughta be grateful to him, instead of accusing him of things he didn't do."

Gemma was trembling now, too. Sera could see it as her sister grasped the pen and scrawled on the paper, *The poems. I really thought he wrote them.*

Sera reluctantly nodded. *Someone* had written the damned things. And when you took into account the fact that Gemma had been seriously injured, had come close to death, had lived with a wired-up jaw for over a month already, maybe it made sense that she'd mistake Ben's professional attention for something else. If you were Gemma, that is, who assumed all men fell for her like dominoes. *Which they usually did.*

"What's become of Jack? Doesn't he come over anymore?"

Gemma shook her head. *Dumped him,* she scribbled.

"Why?"

Gemma shrugged and her face showed rebelliousness.

"Jack was a really great guy, Em."

Gemma's pen bit into the paper. *Old, serious, no fun. Boring.*

Gemma was lying again. Sera gave her a narrow-eyed stare. "Oh, yeah? Seemed to me you two had something good going. What makes you think he didn't write those poems?"

Gemma rolled her eyes as if that was the most ridiculous thing she'd ever heard.

Some demon made Sera say, "Maybe I'll give him a call tomorrow, ask him out for brunch, seeing that you two aren't an item anymore. I really liked him."

A dull flush spread up Gemma's neck and suffused her face. *What about Halsey?* The paper tore under the force of the pen.

"What about him?" Sera raised her eyebrows and prayed that she could lie convincingly. "It's over between us. I told him I didn't want to see him again." She could barely keep from clutching her chest, her heart hurt so much every time she thought of Ben. "It might be fun to get to know Jack better. He's really sexy. Didn't you notice that?"

Gemma shrugged and threw the pen and paper onto the dresser. She climbed into the other twin bed and turned her back to Sera, seemingly indifferent to Sera's words, but her breathing was harsh and heavy.

So Gemma cared about Jack. Sera decided to do exactly what she'd threatened: in the morning, she'd skip church and invite Jack Kilgallin out to brunch, instead. Gemma would be spitting mad, Sera thought with an enormous surge of satisfaction. Well, it was past time her sister got a little of her own medicine.

SERA MET JACK at a local hotel famous for its Sunday buffet brunch. He looked decidedly handsome in a gray sport coat that exactly matched his eyes. He'd been surprised when she'd called, but Sera had counted on the fact that he was too much of a gentleman to refuse her invitation.

They talked about everything except Gemma. Jack asked about her job, and what she thought of living in California. Sera confided that she liked Vancouver better; L.A. was fine, but it wasn't home.

Jack wasn't a verbal man, Sera noticed. Instead, he was a listener, who paid close attention to what his companion said and asked questions that invited long answers. He had a charming way of making a woman feel fascinating.

Sera waited until they'd finished eating to reach into her straw bag and extract the sheets of poetry she'd snuck out of the box in Gemma's bottom drawer. Her sister had made it difficult by staying in bed that morning, refusing to go to church with Aldo and Maria. Sera had waited until Gemma made a hasty trip to the bathroom.

"You wrote these, didn't you, Jack?" Sera prayed that she was right, and her heart lifted when he nodded without bothering to do more than glance at them. A flush spread across his cheekbones, and he carefully avoided meeting her eyes. He was embarrassed.

"Why didn't you tell Gemma you were the one sending them?"

He put sugar into his coffee and stirred it much more than it needed. His voice was strained when he said simply, "She'd have laughed at me."

Sera began to protest and then stopped. He was probably right; her sister might have done exactly that. Sending them anonymously had added intrigue and mystery, which Jack undoubtedly knew would capture Gemma's imagination.

"They're good," she told him honestly. "I guess every kid tries to write poetry at some point. I did, and I remember how hard it was."

"Thanks." His face was still flushed, but now he met her gaze, defiant pride in his eyes. "I've published some in little magazines," he admitted shyly. "Four poems. Nothing big." He reached out and touched the pile of poems with a finger. "But these were private. I wanted to let Gemma know how I really felt about her. But she didn't seem to get the message.'' There was pain in his voice; a longing for a loved one, which Sera recognized.

That he loved her sister wasn't news. Sera thought of how many times he'd brought Gemma flowers and CDs and magazines. She thought again how good-looking he was, how torn apart he'd been when Gemma was injured.

Em was an absolute idiot not to appreciate him.

And, Sera reasoned as she watched the play of emotions on his face, the wonderful thing about Jack was that although he was polite and friendly, Sera could sense that he wasn't at all interested in *her;* the fact that she and Gemma were twins didn't intrigue him in the slightest.

And now she was going to have to hurt him by telling him that Gemma believed Ben had written the poems Jack had sent her so hopefully.

She did it as quickly and clearly as she could, filling in every detail, and by the time she was done, Jack's initial surprise had turned to disgust.

''Between us, it seems we've created one hell of a mess, Gemma and I. I made a mistake by not telling her the poems were from me—I guess I really believed she'd just know. I'm long overdue on setting the record straight with her.''

Sera could hear the steel in his tone. Jack was quiet, but beneath the controlled exterior were passion and strength.

"I like Dr. Halsey," Jack added. "We need to straighten this out right away, for his sake." A muscle clenched and unclenched in his jaw, and rage smoldered in his gray eyes, rage that Sera knew was directed at her sister.

Jack insisted on paying the bill, and then he took the poems and folded them carefully into his jacket pocket. "I'll follow you over to your parents' house right now," he said with a determination that brooked no argument.

Sera wasn't about to protest. She drove straight home, with Jack's sedate blue Pontiac right behind her. Her parents' car wasn't in the driveway; they weren't home from church yet, and Sera was relieved. Getting this first part over without an audience would be easier, Sera decided.

Gemma was drinking coffee in the kitchen, hair unbrushed and wild around her face and shoulders. She was still in her yellow nightshirt. She glanced up sullenly when Sera came in, and then her eyes went huge when she saw Jack.

She jumped to her feet, intending to race out of the room, but Jack caught her arm.

"Sit down." He pulled out a chair and guided her into it. "We have to talk."

Sera caught a glimpse of his eyes, and they were blazing. She knew she probably should leave Gemma and Jack alone, but she couldn't bring herself to walk out of the kitchen. This affected her as well as them; she wanted to know exactly what Jack would say, and how her sister would react.

He reached in his pocket and drew out the poetry, then slapped it down in front of Gemma.

"I wrote these for you, you little fool," he began. "I've been in love with you since the first day you set foot on the construction site, but I can promise you I'm gonna try my best now to get over you, Gemma." The hurt and betrayal he felt were obvious. "I said before you were a spoiled brat, but you're also a dangerous one. Now, tell me the truth. Did Doc Halsey do anything at all to make you think he'd written these?"

Gemma stared at Jack, her eyes huge, and then she slowly shook her head.

Jack swore under his breath. "It's past time you grew up and took responsibility for the things you do," he said in a harsh tone. "You can't hurt people and get away with it. It'll always come back to you, somehow or other."

Sera watched her sister's face crumple, and she couldn't help but feel sorry for her. Plainly, Gemma really cared for Jack—otherwise she'd never have sat this quietly and actually listened.

In fact, by her stricken expression, Sera suspected that Gemma was in love with him, had been all along without realizing it.

"We're gonna straighten this out before I walk out of here, Gemma," Jack continued, his voice hard and determined. "You're gonna tell your dad the truth, and then I'll call Doc Halsey and tell him I wrote the poetry. Maybe you can't talk, but you can sure as hell write him a note saying you were mistaken in what you believed. He can show it to whoever Aldo complained to at the hospital." He grabbed a pen and paper from the counter and slapped them, too, down in front of Gemma.

"Write," he ordered.

Sera held her breath. She knew from past experience that when the moment came for Gemma to make amends for something she'd done, she became hysterical, throwing things, running out of the room, locking herself in the bathroom.

She watched, astounded, as her sister looked up at Jack for what seemed a very long time. He held her gaze, his expression relentless. "It's up to you to make things right, Gemma," he finally said. "You screwed up—you fix it. That's the rule."

Gemma's shoulder's hunched and she bent her head. Tears dripped down her cheeks and fell on the paper, but she slowly picked up the pen.

Sera reached for tissues for her, but Jack had already found some and handed them over.

They all heard the front door open and close.

"Girls, are you coming to Aunt Teresa's?" Maria's heels clicked down the hallway. "She'll be disappointed if you don't—"

She paused in the kitchen doorway. "Hello, Jack,

I thought that was your car outside. It's good to see you again. You can come along and have dinner with us. Teresa always has enough to feed a thousand extra. Sera, I know your flight leaves at four, but Teresa's made cream horns just for you. Visit for a little while and then Papa will drive you to the airport. Gemma, what on earth are you doing still in your nightgown?''

The strained atmosphere finally penetrated, and she fell silent just as Aldo squeezed past her, giving her an affectionate pat on the rump.

"Hello, Jack, good to see you. What's everybody doin' here in the kitchen?''

"There're some things you should know, Aldo.'' Jack motioned to the poetry. "I wrote these, not Doc Halsey.''

Aldo was astounded. "*You* wrote poems?''

Jack's face flushed, but he met Aldo's eyes and nodded. "And Gemma was mistaken when she thought Halsey came on to her, weren't you, Em?''

Once again, still with great reluctance, Gemma nodded.

"He didn't do anything except treat her as his patient. She figures he deserves an apology, so she's writing one.''

Aldo sank onto a chair, and Maria moved over to put a reassuring hand on Gemma's shoulder. She looked at Jack and gave a slow nod of approval.

For a man of few words, Sera thought with admiration, Jack Kilgallin did fine once he got going.

CHAPTER NINETEEN

SERA COULD TELL that her father wasn't as ready as Maria to accept everything Jack was saying. Aldo bent over the table until his face was on a level with Gemma's.

"You *sure, cara,* that the doc didn't do anything to you?"

Gemma didn't look up, but she shook her head.

Aldo, too, shook his head and then swore as he realized the implications of her answer. "How come you said he wrote these, Gemma Cardano?" he asked, picking up the poems and shaking them.

Jack intervened. "The poetry was an honest mistake, Aldo. I should've let her know right from the beginning it was from me."

"Yes, you should have." Maria went over, emptied the grounds from the coffeemaker and refilled it. "But I said all along it wasn't right to jump to conclusions. Now we have to deal with the consequences." She reached for telephone. "I'll phone Teresa and let her know we'll be late." She dialed and spoke rapidly to her sister-in-law. When she was finished she gave the receiver to her husband.

"Okay, Aldo, now you get hold of Dr. Halsey," she ordered. "The sooner this is cleared up, the better."

Aldo was obviously reluctant to admit how wrong he'd been, but he finally shrugged and nodded.

"I have Ben's pager number. That'll probably be the best way to contact him." Sera fished her wallet out of her bag and handed over the number. "I'm going up to pack my things. I think I'll just take a cab out to the airport."

She didn't want to be around when her father spoke to Ben. Knowing he was on the other end of the telephone would be too hard to bear. And if he asked again to speak to her, having to refuse would be agonizing.

Maria began to protest the cab idea, but Sera was firm. "There isn't really time for me to come to Aunt Teresa's, Mama. Besides, I want to call Maisie. I told her I'd be in town this weekend, and we haven't had a chance to visit. I'm gonna see if maybe she'll drive out and meet me for a coffee at the airport." Sera didn't add that she needed a strong shoulder to cry on.

"I can drive you out," Jack offered. "I'll be leaving as soon as we talk to the doctor."

Sera saw the stricken expression on Gemma's face and knew she had to do something for her sister.

"Thanks, Jack. You don't mind if Gemma comes along to see me off?" she improvised. Again she was counting on Jack's good manners. She hoped he was too polite to refuse Gemma a ride, especially in front of her mother and father.

Jack shot her a furious, accusing look, but after a moment he reluctantly nodded. "Okay, and I'll bring her home."

"You finished that letter, Em?" Without waiting for an answer, Sera grabbed her sister's hand and dragged her to her feet. "C'mon upstairs and get some clothes on."

If traffic was heavy, driving back from the airport would take over an hour, and Gemma and Jack would be alone in his car. Whether Gemma was able to talk or not, Sera was banking on her sister weaseling past Jack's anger to somehow find a way to let him know she loved him.

Sera was determined to spell out to Gemma what she had to do, just in case it hadn't occurred to her. After all, they were twins. Sera truly wanted Gemma to have a chance at happiness.

At least one of them should come out of this fiasco with the man she loved.

BEN WATCHED Grendel race across the sand toward the seagulls and scatter them into the sky. He'd driven to this deserted stretch of beach to try to come to terms with his life, but it wasn't working.

Maybe he'd feel better when he knew Sera's flight had taken off. For some obscure reason he'd called the airport to find out what time the flights to San Diego left this afternoon. There were two, one at four and one at eleven. He was fairly certain she'd take the earlier flight, so it wouldn't be long now before she was gone.

Scuffing the sand beneath his bare feet, he headed after Grendel, mentally listing the things that had gone so wrong in the past week.

His dream of receiving a sessional appointment as head of St. Joe's new burn unit was dashed. Oh, he had no doubt that even if formal charges were brought against him, he'd eventually establish his innocence, but the notoriety surrounding any suggestion of sexual misconduct would be enough to prejudice the board against his appointment.

Strangely enough, though, that wasn't what was causing him the most anguish. It was losing Sera that made him feel his life was pointless.

He picked up a stone and threw it out into the water, and Grendel yelped with joy and went plunging into the surf after it. Ben shook his head. Damn dog didn't know the difference between a stone and a rubber ball. Well, he was like his master in that area. Ben had taken long enough to recognize love when it had finally appeared.

He'd changed drastically since he'd met Sera, Ben mused, letting the waves wash over his feet and ankles. He could see now what was important, and it wasn't his career as he'd always believed. He'd been certain that it came first in his life, but he knew now that conviction was just one of the defenses he'd erected to keep himself safe from loving.

He stopped suddenly as a new thought struck him. If his career wasn't the center of his life, what did it matter where he worked? Once he'd passed his state board examinations in California, he could probably get a job in a clinic in L.A. or even San Diego; his qualifications were excellent. That idea lifted his spirits, but they plummeted again immediately.

What good would it do him to be in California if Sera really meant what she said, that she didn't want to see or hear from him again? She'd sounded adamant enough when he'd called her last evening.

So why didn't he believe her? Was it simply his male ego that had him convinced she cared in spite of what she said?

He'd never told her he loved her, he remembered with disgust. He'd never said he wanted to get married, either.

A large wave came rolling in and crested at his feet, soaking him. He barely felt it.

The thought of marriage hadn't entered his head until this exact moment, and it scared the living hell out of him. But it also felt exactly right. He did want to marry Sera. He wanted to have babies with her, like Hannah, like Stanley. He wanted to grow old with her at his side, but it wasn't going to happen unless he did something fast.

He glanced at his watch. There was a way to settle this, once and for all. He'd have to break the speed limit.

"Grendel. Grendel, come on. Hurry it up."

She'd have left for the airport already. He had to catch her before she boarded her flight. He lifted the wet, salty dog in his arms and hurriedly strapped him into the back of the truck.

He'd deliberately left his pager on the seat, and he glanced at it as he started the engine. Habit made him check it. He'd missed four calls, all from the same number, and his heart leaped when he recognized it; someone had been phoning him from the Cardanos' house.

It could only have been Sera. He dialed her cell number as he steered out of the parking lot, and then he disconnected before it had a chance to ring.

He was through communicating with her by phone. Whatever she had to say would be said in person this time, so he could watch her eyes and know the truth.

Using every shortcut and keeping a careful eye on the rearview mirror for cops, he sped toward the airport.

WEARY AND DRAINED of emotion, Sera stood in the long line waiting to go through Customs. Maisie had offered to wait with her, but Sera had insisted her friend leave after their quick coffee in the cafeteria; Maisie had a date, and from the way she sounded and looked when she talked about James he was obviously someone special.

"He owns a restaurant. Can you imagine anything more dangerous for my weight than to be with a guy who loves to cook?" But she was glowing, and she couldn't seem to stop smiling. She managed to bring James's name into their conversation a dozen times in imaginative ways that finally even coaxed a smile from Sera.

Maisie had also insisted there was a job on the set of the new movies soon to be shot, if Sera wanted it.

"Pasquale's okay for the short-term, but he's pretty unpredictable," Maisie said. "You can have a job one day, and the next he'll have a fight with the director and the entire crew will be out on their ear."

Pasquale *was* difficult to work with, as Sera had learned. From a career standpoint, to come back to Vancouver made the best sense. But from a sanity standpoint, being in the same city with Ben was simply too much of a temptation. She'd planned to spill out the whole mixed-up story to Maisie, but in the end she hadn't.

"I knew you had a major thing for the doc," Maisie said. "Why not come back and give him another chance."

"Because it wouldn't work." Sera hadn't had the energy to go into the complicated saga of what had happened between her and Ben, and she was relieved that Maisie didn't pursue it.

"Just be really sure before you blow up all your bridges," was the only advice Maisie offered.

And she *was* sure, Sera told herself, wearily pushing her suitcase along with her foot as the long line inched forward. It was just too bad her head and her heart weren't in sync.

She was three people from the head of the line when she heard her name being called. She recognized Ben's voice instantly and whirled around.

He was shouldering his way through the crowd, oblivious to the resentful looks and nasty protests of those around him. He was wearing decrepit olive-green cutoffs and a sleeveless blue T-shirt covered with dog hair. Behind him, he dragged a reluctant Grendel on a leash that kept getting wound around people's baggage and legs, and from the way both he and Grendel were panting when they finally reached her, they'd obviously been running hard.

Ben's glasses were filthy, Sera noted; that he could see out of them at all was a wonder.

"Sera." He was sweating and there were dark

perspiration marks under each arm and across his chest.

"Sera, I have to ask you something."

The people behind her grumbled as Grendel scrambled over their suitcases. When he got close enough, she bent over and rubbed his ears. The dog smelled high and felt wet. He put both paws up on Sera.

"Grendel, get off her." Ben shoved the dog down and took her hand between both of his. "Listen, I've had an idea. I could move to San Diego and get a job," he puffed. "Or L.A.—they always need good plastic surgeons in L.A. What d'ya think, Sera?" He drew in a deep breath and added as an afterthought, "We could get married. Whenever you're ready. You'd probably want to wait a week or two for that, but that's fine with me."

Married? *Married?* How had he gone from no commitment to marriage with nothing in between? And what was he doing here, at this very last minute?

"Did my mother talk to you?" Of course Maria had guessed how Sera felt about Ben. Dear God, what had Mama told him?

"Your mother?" Ben frowned and shook his head. "Nope, I haven't spoken to any of your family. My lawyer told me not to."

"Your lawyer?"

"Yeah, she figured your dad might be a little confrontational. She said not to speak to anybody."

"Papa didn't call you?"

"No. Listen, Sera, this is about you and me. We can discuss your family after, okay?"

Aldo hadn't managed to reach him. Ben didn't know that the complaints against him would be withdrawn. He needed to know those things.

"You're next, lady. You're holding up the line." The elderly U.S. Customs official behind the desk had a booming voice and he was scowling at her, and Sera automatically reached for her suitcase. Ben snatched it from her and Grendel tried to block her way, but Sera moved forward anyway.

"There's another flight to San Diego tonight at eleven," Ben babbled, following her with Grendel and her suitcase in tow. "Let's go over to the ticket counter and I'll book you on that one. We absolutely need time to talk this out."

"Could I see your passport and ticket, please?" The official held out his hand and Sera passed over the documents. Things were happening too quickly. She couldn't figure out what was best to do. Grendel was now lying across her shoes, making it nearly impossible to move.

"Please, Sera." Ben sounded desperate. "Cut me some slack here, okay? I talked to Vera. I finally realized I was the one who needed to get on with my life."

"So he's been two-timing you, huh? You're better off without him." By now the Customs man was interested. "C'mon through, miss," he bellowed. "Let this guy stew in his own juice."

Ben glared at him. "I happen to love this woman," he stated. "I'm trying to explain myself here, and you're not helping."

"Is he on the level, or has he really messed you up?" When Sera didn't answer the man turned on Ben. "We have rules in this country, y'know. Two strikes and you're out, son."

Sera ignored him, but her face burned, because now everyone nearby was listening. The official might as well have had a megaphone.

"What if there're no seats on the next flight, Ben? I have to be back at work in the morning."

"There're always seats in executive class. I'll make sure you get on the plane."

Should she trust him? Sera thought of Maisie and blowing up bridges, and she stuck her hand out for her documents. "Sorry, sir. I've changed my mind. I'll take the later flight."

"I only hope that's a wise decision," the Customs man said, and then he relented and grinned at her. "He seems not a bad fellow. We all make mistakes." He winked at Ben and roared, "Better make it good, son."

Ben did his best. Within fifteen minutes, he'd managed to get Sera a seat on the eleven o'clock flight. He put her suitcase in a locker, handed over her tickets and key and then led her and Grendel out of the cavernous departures lounge and into the late-afternoon sunlight. He found an empty bench by a bus stop and they sat down.

"I want to explain everything," Ben began, but she interrupted him.

While he was busy with tickets and baggage, Sera had had time to think. "Ben, I have to tell you what's been going on today, why my father was calling you."

Grendel sat on his haunches beside her, his head and one dirty paw in the lap of her silk-nub slacks. She stroked him as she related the whole story, being careful to include every sordid detail. She rested her hand on the dog's warm head, wishing that love was as simple for her as it was for Grendel.

"That's why Papa's been calling you," she concluded. "He wants to apologize both to you and to the guy at the hospital. Gemma's also written you a letter of apology. It's all over, Ben. So you see, there's no problem with your career. You'll still get that job you want so much."

She held her breath, trying to shield her heart, trying not to hope or believe. He'd retract everything now that his job was secure again. Things would go back to what they had always been for him.

He was holding her hand, and she waited, expecting him to give it an apologetic squeeze and then release it, release her. She waited, steeling herself against the hurt.

Grendel whined and Ben said in a quiet voice, "Do you think you could love me, Sera?"

Nervousness turned to irritation. Why did he have to ask that? She'd been avoiding his gaze, looking down at Grendel, but now she looked full at Ben, knowing that it didn't matter what she said, because the truth was written in her eyes, on her face, and she was weary of trying to hide it.

Even so, she needed courage to voice it.

"I already do." She gulped. "Love you."

He expelled a long sigh, and his voice was less than steady. "I'm glad. I'm so glad. Because I love you, too, Sera Cardano. And I intend to spend the rest of my life with you, and I don't give a damn where we spend it. Vancouver's okay. California's nice." The smile that lit up his face was luminous, filled with joy, triumphant, and it seemed to spread over and through her until there was not the slightest space left in her heart for doubt.

Neither was there space for Grendel as Ben wrapped his arms around her, pulling her close to him, ignoring the dog's yelp of protest.

Sera carefully removed Ben's filthy glasses and clung to him, wrapping her arms around his neck. She'd tell him later on that she didn't want him to move to California. She'd tell him she'd much rather work with Maisie right here in Vancouver. They could live in his loft, at least until they had babies. Oh, she wanted his babies.

There would always be Gemma to cope with, of course. Things hadn't appeared too hopeful between Gemma and Jack when they drove away from the airport together; Jack had looked grim and Gemma had looked frantic.

Ben and Aldo would have to shake hands and be friends.

And Ben hadn't even met all her relatives yet; Sera suspected that at least three of her aunts would hit him up for a face-lift once he was part of the family.

She'd discuss it all with him, eventually.

But right now she couldn't say a word because she was being thoroughly kissed by the man she intended to marry.

EPILOGUE

"IT'S GOING to be a white Christmas, Ben, isn't that perfect?"

Sera was jubilant. The rain that had pelted Vancouver for the past week had miraculously changed to snow just as darkness was falling, and tomorrow was Christmas Eve.

"Is this straight, love?" Ben, perched precariously on a paint ladder, carefully settled the angel on the top of the eight-foot Christmas tree Sera had insisted upon. "Make sure, because I'm not climbing up here again—I don't fancy the idea of spending Christmas in the ER as a patient."

"It's beautiful. Come down and look."

"Gladly. Gratefully. And I'm hiring someone to dismantle this when Christmas is over." Ben stepped gingerly down and together they contemplated the glimmering tree.

"You're right, sweetheart." He looped an arm around her shoulders and gave her a squeeze. "The tree's absolutely spectacular. Stanley's gonna flip out when he sees it."

She'd positioned the immense tree so it reflected

in the wall-size mirror. There appeared to be two Christmas trees, ablaze with hundreds of tiny golden lights, and now that it was dark outside, the entire room was also reproduced in the glass of the window wall.

"I think everything's almost ready. We just need to finish wrapping the presents," Sera said, casting a critical eye around the main floor of the loft. The soft taupe walls and the rich, darkly exotic rugs set the stage for the groupings of comfortably over-stuffed couches and armchairs and low tables, an eclectic mix of old and new that she'd chosen to furnish the huge space. Green plants flourished in odd corners; pottery bowls on low tables held out-size acorns; and harvest baskets overflowed with holly and colored glass balls. On the walls, Ben's drawings mingled happily with framed Gauguin prints, and underneath the skylight, situated just where the afternoon light was the best, stood the long worktable she and Ben shared. He painted or sculpted while she constructed the models for her sets. The lifelike busts of Stanley and baby Hannah that he'd finished and cast in bronze as gifts for Greg and Lily sat on the table, waiting to be boxed.

"We'll put the turkey in the oven as soon as we get up in the morning," Sera plotted. "I tried it. It fits, but just barely. And there'll probably be tons of food because everybody's bringing their specialty. Aunt Teresa's making cream horns and Uncle Dino's sure to cook up that awful lentil soup of his. He laces it with so much brandy it's not safe for the kids to eat.''

Ben grinned, aware that Sera was more than a little nervous about the party they'd planned for Christmas Eve; this was the first time they'd be entertaining formally, and the guest list had quickly grown to astronomical proportions.

After their wedding in mid-September, Sera had elected to spend her honeymoon decorating the loft. They could go on a trip later, she'd insisted, which made sense, because both she and he were unusually busy with their careers.

Sera was working with Maisie on the challenging sets for a horror movie, and Ben had been invited by the hospital board to supervise the final planning for the burn unit, which would open the following summer. The invitation meant that his sessional appointment as head was almost a certainty.

Sera had been in her element as painters transformed the walls and ceilings of the loft and muscled deliverymen obediently arranged furniture to her specifications.

Ben smiled now at the memory. He and Grendel had done their heroic best to be enthusiastic and supportive about the redecorating, but their apprehension had been all too evident to his wife. She'd lavished affection on them to offset the trauma of it all, a situation they'd taken shameful advantage of. He'd actually been a little sorry when the loft was finished, and he was convinced Grendel felt the same.

"Gemma finally found a wedding dress," Sera announced, moving away from him to plump up the goose-down cushions on the sofa and straighten an ornament on the tree. "It's off-white, with Empire styling to hide her big belly."

They both laughed. Gemma had managed to get pregnant last August, and she was having twins. Ben and Sera had wickedly speculated that it must have happened the very day Jack had driven Sera to the airport.

True to her contrary self, Gemma had refused to be hurried into marriage. She'd insisted she wanted a long engagement, and Jack had patiently indulged her, until December arrived and her stomach began to reach monumental proportions. Then he'd firmly set the wedding date for New Year's Eve. Ben noted that Gemma hadn't argued.

Ben's own relationship with Gemma was still uncomfortably strained. Much as he wanted to, he didn't trust her; he'd still prefer not to be in her company, but Maria stubbornly insisted her daughters and their partners come to family dinners every single week. Ben was trying, but he doubted the time would ever arrive when he'd be able to totally forgive Sera's sister.

Sera never mentioned it to him, but Ben instinctively knew his feelings about her sister troubled her. Gemma was, after all, her twin.

Aldo, too, had been awkward and uneasy with Ben until the September afternoon when Maria and her daughters were busy preparing for Sera's wedding, arguing together over flowers and invitations and dresses and food and hairstyles.

In self-defense, Ben and Aldo had taken refuge in front of the television. They watched two soccer matches and somehow drank their way through a large bottle of *grappa,* a lethal homemade Italian liquor. As the *grappa* dwindled, conversation flowed, and by the time the bottle was empty, they were firm friends. Ben was almost sure the killer hangover he'd suffered the following day was worth it.

Ben put a Christmas-music CD on the player and turned out lamps until only the tree lights illuminated the room.

Sera was still fussing over the party. "Do you think we've got enough ice?" She was making a list of what needed to be done. "And cranberries—I hope I've got enough cranberry sauce."

Ben took the pad and pen out of her hand and tugged her to her feet. "Forget cranberries. Come and dance with your husband, Mrs. Halsey."

Wrapped in each other's arms, they moved slowly and sensuously as the music played. The second CD was still Christmas music, but with a more lively rock-and-roll beat.

"You up to this, Doctor?" Sera did some intricate footwork, and Ben spun her out and caught her again.

Grendel chose that moment to wake up and come galloping across the room toward them, barking with excitement. He seemed to think he was missing out on some wonderful new game. He tried to insinuate himself between them, and when that didn't work, he growled and nipped at Ben's ankles.

"Stop it, Grendel. Go back and lie down." Ben was perturbed. The dog ignored him, half tripping both of them.

Sera started to giggle helplessly and they collapsed on a couch. "Maybe this is a better idea after all," Ben murmured, trapping her beneath him and nibbling at her neck. "Have I told you lately that I love you, sweetheart?"

"Not for a couple of hours," she said, squirming into a more comfortable position beside him. They lay in each other's arms, looking up at the tree.

He held her against him, aware of her flesh touching his, her warm breath mingling with his own. He'd make hot, sweet love to her tonight, but not quite yet. One of the things he liked about being married was having time.

They'd talked it over, and decided to wait a year

or so before they had babies. They needed an interval to be alone, to focus only on each other, sharing admiration, understanding, trust, desire...and love, such incredible love.

There wasn't any need to rush, because their life waited for them, rich and profound, filled with times of joy and, inevitably, as well, Ben suspected, times of sorrow.

Whatever fate held, they'd weather it together.

"The angel is blessing us," Sera whispered, and Ben nodded, his heart filling up with gratitude, for his life, his beloved Sera and then, taking him completely by surprise, for her sister.

It was only because of Gemma that he'd found Sera.

The revelation was so surprising that Ben threw back his head and laughed, and all the lingering resentment he'd felt toward Gemma melted away.

Sera laughed with him, happy because he was happy, and Grendel leaped up, paws on the couch, to lather their faces with his tongue.

HARLEQUIN®
SUPERROMANCE®

*Pregnant and alone—
these stories follow women
from the heartache of
betrayal to finding true love
and starting a family.*

THE FOURTH CHILD by **C.J. Carmichael.**
When Claire's marriage is in trouble, she tries to
save it—although she's not sure she can forgive her
husband's betrayal.
On sale May 2000.

AND BABY MAKES SIX by **Linda Markowiak.**
Jenny suddenly finds herself jobless and pregnant by
a man who doesn't want their child.
On sale June 2000.

MOM'S THE WORD by **Roz Denny Fox.**
After her feckless husband steals her inheritance and
leaves town with another woman, Hayley discovers she's
pregnant.
On sale July 2000.

Available wherever Harlequin books are sold.

HARLEQUIN®
Makes any time special ™

Visit us at www.eHarlequin.com

HSR9ML01

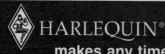

HARLEQUIN®
SUPERROMANCE®

Twins

They're definitely not two of a kind!

THE UNKNOWN SISTER
by
Rebecca Winters

Catherine Casey is an identical twin—and she doesn't know it! When she meets her unknown sister, Shannon White, she discovers they've fallen in love with the same man....

On sale May 2000 wherever Harlequin books are sold.

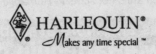

HARLEQUIN®
Makes any time special ™